Praise for Marie Ferrarella:

"A joy to read."
—*RT Book Reviews* on *Christmas Cowboy Duet*

"Ferrarella's romance will charm with all the benefits and pitfalls of a sweet small-town setting."
—*RT Book Reviews* on *Lassoed by Fortune*

"Heartwarming. That's the way I have described every book by Marie Ferrarella that I have read. *In the Family Way* engenders in me the same warm, fuzzy feeling that I have come to expect from her books."
—*The Romance Reader*

"Ms. Ferrarella warms our hearts with her charming characters and delicious interplay."
—*RT Book Reviews* on *A Husband Waiting to Happen*

"Ms. Ferrarella creates fiery, strong-willed characters, an intense conflict and an absorbing premise no reader could possibly resist."
—*RT Book Reviews* on *A Match for Morgan*

Dear Reader,

Every time I finish a set of books revolving around the citizens in Forever, Texas, I am certain that I've exhausted my supply of ideas for that little town. And then (mercifully), a thought, idea, passing comment, news clip, etc., will go by and something happens.

It's a little like Jack and his magic beans in *Jack and the Beanstalk*. The beans get tossed on the ground and suddenly, they just take root and start to grow. This time around, my idea came from inside my mailbox. I am the target for every single charity known to man. I began by sending pennies when I was twelve to a charity trying to provide adequate food, clothing and schooling to Native American children in a reservation school in South Dakota.

Over the years, that has spread to more tribes, more children (St. Jude Hospital—loved Danny Thomas—Shriners' Hospital, etc.) and dogs of various breeds (O.C. German Shepherd Rescue Society, etc.) were included. The one that popped up this particular day was a charity that took in at-risk teens and preteens.

From there to Jackson and Garrett White Eagle's The Healing Ranch was a very short hop, skip and a jump away. I hope you enjoy reading the results as much as I did writing them.

As always, I thank you for taking the time to read this book—something I *never* take for granted. And from the bottom of my heart, I wish you someone to love who loves you back.

All the best,

Marie Ferrarella

THE COWBOY AND THE LADY

MARIE FERRARELLA

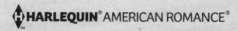
HARLEQUIN® AMERICAN ROMANCE®

Recycling programs
for this product may
not exist in your area.

ISBN-13: 978-0-373-75583-7

The Cowboy and the Lady

Copyright © 2015 by Marie Rydzynski-Ferrarella

Printed in U.S.A.

This *USA TODAY* bestselling and RITA® Award-winning author has written more than two hundred and fifty books for Harlequin, some under the name Marie Nicole. Her romances are beloved by fans worldwide. Visit her website, marieferrarella.com.

Books by Marie Ferrarella

Harlequin American Romance

Forever, Texas

The Sheriff's Christmas Surprise
Ramona and the Renegade
The Doctor's Forever Family
Lassoing the Deputy
A Baby on the Ranch
A Forever Christmas
His Forever Valentine
A Small Town Thanksgiving
The Cowboy's Christmas Surprise
Her Forever Cowboy
Cowboy for Hire

Harlequin Special Edition

Matchmaking Mamas

Wish Upon a Matchmaker
Dating for Two
Diamond in the Ruff

Other titles by this author available in ebook format.

To
Stella Bagwell,
who I always channel
when I go to Texas in my mind.
Thank you for your eternal patience,
and most of all, for your friendship.

Prologue

"You're going where?" John Kincannon demanded angrily.

A high school basketball coach, Deborah Winters Kincannon's husband had just come home to find her shaken and pale as she was terminating a phone call. Her next words to him had obviously taken him by surprise.

From the look on his face, it was rather an unpleasant surprise.

He glared at her. It was supposed to make her back down. But she couldn't. Not this time. If she did, she had a strong feeling the results would turn out to be fatal, if not now, then soon.

Debi felt almost numb as she replaced the receiver on the kitchen wall phone. Part of her refused to believe that the conversation she had just had was real, that it wasn't the product of some recurring nightmare she just couldn't seem to wake up from.

Another part of her knew that this was all too real—and something, frankly, she had been expecting even as she'd been dreading it.

When her husband didn't seem to absorb what she'd said to him, Debi repeated it. "I'm going down to the police station to bail Ryan out."

The simple statement—voiced for a second time—infused her husband with pure rage. His complexion actually reddened as he shifted, blocking her path to the front door.

"Oh, no, you're not," he declared heatedly. "This is it! I have *had* it with that kid, Deborah."

For a second, Debi closed her eyes, digging deep for patience. She wasn't up to another argument. She'd gotten home just ten minutes ago herself, after putting in a very long day in the OR with three back-to-back surgeries. It wasn't supposed to have been three, but one of the other surgical nurses had called in sick and she had wound up pulling an extra shift.

She was bone weary and this was just the absolute *very* last thing she needed to cap off a day that had dragged on much too long.

"Look, I know you're angry," Debi began wearily, "but—"

"No, uh-uh, no 'buts,'" John informed her firmly as well as loudly. "We've given that kid every chance and it's gotten us nowhere. He can stay in that jail and rot for all I care. You're not going down there to bail him out. I refuse to allow it, do you hear me?"

Debi looked at her husband, stunned. Had John always been this hard-hearted and she'd just missed it?

Upset and overwrought, Debi upbraided herself, knowing she had turned a blind eye to one too many signs when it came to John. He'd changed. This was *not* the man she had fallen in love with all those years ago on the campus.

"I can't just leave him there, John," she pointed out, struggling to curb her own anger.

John obviously didn't share her opinion. "You can and

you will," he informed her. "I think I've been pretty understanding about all this. It's not everybody who'll take his wife's brother into his home, but this is it, the proverbial straw. I don't want that kid in my house anymore!"

He was doing it again. John was making her feel like an outsider in her own home. A home she had helped pay for as much as he had. Why was he behaving like a Neanderthal?

"It's my house, too, John," she reminded him, her voice tight.

"Nobody said it wasn't," he snapped at her. "But you're going to have to choose, Deborah."

"Choose?" she repeated incredulously, her voice deadly still. John couldn't possibly be saying what she thought he was saying to her.

When had he gotten so cold, so unfeeling?

There were tears gathering in her soul, but her eyes remained dry.

"Yeah. *Choose*," he emphasized. "It's either Ryan or me, Deborah. You can't have both."

She stared at the man she'd loved all through high school and college. The man she thought she knew so well, but obviously didn't know at all.

Just to be perfectly clear, she put the question to him. "You're asking me to choose between my kid brother and you."

John continued to glare at her. His brown eyes were completely cold and flat, his stand unwavering. "That's what I'm doing."

"Ryan doesn't have anybody but me." Had John forgotten that?

It had only been three short years since Ryan and her parents had been involved in that horrific car accident. He was twelve at the time. The accident claimed her parents and came very close to claiming her brother, as well. It had taken close to six months of physical therapy before Ryan could get back on his feet.

The scars on his body healed. The ones inside his head were another story. Debi was convinced that they were responsible for her brother transforming from a kind, sweet young man who got straight As into a sullen, troubled teen who ditched more classes than he attended.

"That's not my problem," John informed her. "Him or me, Deborah. You have to choose."

If he could say that to her, then their marriage was already over, she realized. "I'm not leaving him in jail, John," she retorted, grabbing up her shoulder bag.

"Fine. Go." John angrily waved her toward the door. "Rescue that sad sack of wasted flesh. But when you get back, I won't be here."

Angry, hurt and exasperated beyond words that John could put her into this sort of a position when she was struggling to deal with the circumstances surrounding her brother's arrest, she glared at her husband. "That is *your* choice, John. I can't do anything about that," she informed him coldly.

"You're making a big mistake, Deborah!" John shouted at her back.

She squared her shoulders. "I think I made one four years ago," Debi said, referring to the length of their marriage. She didn't bother to turn around. She slammed the door in her wake, thinking that it might make her feel better.

It didn't.

She had a confused, rebellious younger brother who was, unless something drastic happened, on his way to a serious prison record before his eighteenth birthday, and a husband who was bailing on her at the worst possible time rather than offering emotional support.

She had hit rock bottom, Debi thought as she got into her car and started up the engine. Worse than that, she was in far over her head. What she desperately needed was to find a way back up to the surface before she drowned.

Chapter One

Standing just inside the corral, Jackson White Eagle leaned back against the recently repainted railing, watching three of the current crop of teenage boys, who lived in the old converted bunkhouse, put the horses through their paces.

They probably didn't realize that in actuality the horses were putting *them* through *their* paces, Jackson thought. Training horses trained *them*.

He felt the corners of his mouth curve just a little in satisfaction.

Whatever the reason behind it, even after all this time, it still felt odd to glance in a mirror or a reflecting window and realize that he was smiling. The first ten or so years of his life, there had been precious little for him to smile about. He had grown up with nothing but bitter words and anger erupting, time and again, in his house.

His parents were always fighting. His father, Ben White Eagle, was a great deal larger than his mother and Jackson had instinctively taken his mother's side. He'd appointed himself her protector even though at ten, he had been small for his age and his father had continually referred to him as "a worthless runt."

Despite that demoralizing image, he had tried his best

to protect the woman who had given him life. He went on being protective of his mother until the day that she walked out on his father —and him.

At first, he had convinced himself that it was just an oversight on her part. He'd told himself that his mother was too angry at his father to realize that she'd left without him.

Night after night, he waited, listening for her return.

But after two weeks had passed, and then three, and then four, he knew he had to face the truth. His mother wasn't coming back for him. That forced him to face the fact that the person who he had loved most in the world hadn't loved him enough to take him with her. His heart broke.

And then he just shut down.

By then, four weeks after his mother had taken off, his father was already preparing to get married again. He was marrying the woman he'd been having an affair with. The affair that had produced another son and had been the final straw for his first wife.

Like him, his stepmother, Sylvia, was only half Navajo. Sylvia was also the mother of his half brother, Garrett, who was five at the time of his parents' marriage.

The second his father brought Sylvia into the house, Jackson was certain that he was going to be locked out of the family. In his eyes, his father, Sylvia and Garrett formed a complete unit. That left him in the role of the outsider, unwanted and on the outside, looking in.

But Sylvia hadn't been the typical stepmother he'd expected. To his surprise, she reached out to him. She went so far as to tell him that she wasn't going to try to take his mother's place. But that didn't mean that he couldn't come to her with anything that was bothering him. Knowing that he'd gone through a lot, she said that she intended to be there for him, as well as for Garrett. To her, they were *both* her sons.

He'd appreciated the effort on Sylvia's part, but he was just too angry at the world, predominantly his mother, to allow Sylvia into his life. He began acting out, taking part in unacceptable behavior.

Things went from bad to worse.

His father's idea of fixing a problem was to take a belt to the cause. At first, he did it covertly, waiting until he got Jackson alone. But he soon tired of that and lashed out at him the moment his temper flared.

The first time Sylvia became aware of what her husband was doing, she quickly put herself between him and Jackson. Ben had shoved her aside, which caused Jackson to attempt to tackle him. It ended badly for Jackson, but he had gotten a few licks in before his father had gotten the better of him.

Sylvia had called the reservation police. Ben White Eagle took off for parts unknown that same night, before they came for him.

Jackson was relieved that his father was gone, but the absence of his father's salary made life very difficult for Sylvia, his half brother and him. Sylvia never blamed him, never threw the incident in his face. This didn't change the fact that he felt as if he was to blame for everything that had gone wrong.

Things got even worse.

He got arrested—more than once. And each time he did, Sylvia would go to the local law enforcement establishment on the reservation, pay whatever fines needed to be paid and bring him back home.

Jackson secretly felt sorry for what he was putting her

through, but even her tears hadn't gotten him to change. Angry at the world and with little to no self-esteem to speak of, for a while it looked as if his fate was predestined—and cast in stone.

And then his stepmother, in what she later admitted to him was one final act of desperation, turned to his father's older and far sterner, as well as far more stable, brother, Sam, for help. Sam White Eagle had pulled himself out of poverty and had, Jackson later found out, managed to survive personal tragedy, as well, although at the time it had been touch and go. His wife of less than eighteen months died giving birth to his son. Beset by a number of complications, the baby had died a couple of days later. Sam had them buried together. And then he had shut himself down emotionally, losing himself in bottle after bottle until he finally pulled himself up out of what he recognized would have been a death spiral.

Emotionally stoic, he did feel for his brother's sons as well as for Sylvia, which led to his taking her up on her plea.

Sam became the male role model for both him and for Garrett. Initially, his uncle put them both to work on his small horse ranch. His reasoning was that if they were kept constantly busy, they wouldn't have the time, not to mention the energy, to act out.

His uncle turned out to be right. Jackson knew that to the end of his days, no matter what he accomplished, he would owe it all to Sam. When his uncle died, leaving the ranch to him and to Garrett, Jackson decided that Sam's work should continue. He broached the idea to Garrett, who didn't need to be sold on it. His brother wholeheartedly agreed with him before he'd had a chance to finish a second sentence.

And that was how The Healing Ranch came to be. Five years after Sam had passed away, the ranch was still in existence, turning out top-quality quarter horses and transformed juvenile offenders who had learned to walk the straight and narrow.

Secretly, Jackson had thought that, after a while, this so-called crusade he had undertaken would get old for him. When he had first started all this, he hadn't realized that there was a part of him that actually enjoyed the challenge, that looked forward to that rush that came when he knew that the misdirected kid he was working with had turned a corner and no longer was interested in gaining notoriety for what he did wrong but for what he did that was right.

"Wish you were here, Sam, to see this," Jackson murmured under his breath. He glanced up at the all but cloudless sky. "This is all your doing, you know," he added.

"You know, they lock people up who talk to themselves with such feeling," Garrett said to his older brother as he came over to join him.

Five years younger than Jackson, and with only their father in common, the whole world could still easily identify the two as brothers. They almost looked alike, from their deep, thick, blue-black hair to their hypnotic blue eyes. Jackson's had come directly from his mother while with Garrett it was most likely someone somewhere within his family tree.

"Just your word against mine, Garrett. No one else is anywhere within earshot so there's no one around to back up your claim. They'll think you just want the ranch all to yourself and that you're looking for a way to get me out of the picture," Jackson told him.

So saying, Jackson eyed his half brother. They had gone through a lot together, he thought with affection. That didn't mean that either of them ever purposely missed a chance to zing the other.

Garrett grinned. "I guess you saw right through my plot." He snapped his fingers like someone acknowledging a missed opportunity. "Foiled again. Looks like I'm just going to have to come up with another way to take over the old homestead."

Jackson glanced at his watch. The latest applicant he had accepted at the beginning of the week should have arrived by now. He wondered if something had happened to bring about a change in plans. It wouldn't be the first time a teen's parent or guardian had backed out of the arrangement before it ever started. Total commitment was required and sometimes that didn't pan out.

"I take it there's no word yet on our latest resident 'bad boy'?" he asked Garrett.

Heaven help him, he needed a new challenge, Jackson thought. Needed to be given another teen to turn around and thereby rescue. With each and every one that he and Garrett rehabilitated, he was paying off a little more of the debt that he owed to Sam, a debt that he could never really fully repay. And although his uncle had been gone for a few years now, Jackson felt that somehow, Sam knew the good that was being done in his name by the boy he had saved from coming to a very an unsavory end.

Garrett climbed onto the corral, straddling the top rail.

"Not yet," he answered. "I just checked phone messages, emails and text messages. Unless the kid and his guardian are using smoke signals to communicate, they haven't tried to get in touch with us." Garrett shrugged casually. "Could be they just decided to change their minds at the last minute."

"Always possible," Jackson admitted—although he really doubted it. The call he had received from the troubled teen's guardian made him feel that the woman thought that the situation was desperate—just as desperate as she was. He'd heard things in her voice that she hadn't knowingly put into words, but he'd heard them just the same. Things that told him that even if he didn't have a ready bed for this latest applicant, he would have found a way to make room somehow.

Luckily, he hadn't had to get creative on that front. When he'd inherited the ranch, he and Garrett had renovated the bunkhouse so that it could handle eight boys with ease. Ten would have necessitated bringing in two extra twin beds and space would have been rather limited, but it could be done.

Currently, there were seven boys living on the ranch besides Garrett and himself. His latest success story, Casey Brooks, had graduated less than a week ago. Upon his initial arrival, Casey had been one seriously messed-up, lost sixteen-year-old. His parents had gotten in contact with him because they were genuinely afraid that their son would either be killed or eventually land in prison, where heaven only knew what would happen to him.

Casey had been so tightly wound up it was a wonder he hadn't just exploded before he ever came to The Healing Ranch.

Getting through to the inner, hidden, decent teen had required an extreme amount of patience and going not just the extra mile but the extra twenty miles. There were times when he was certain that Casey was just too far gone to reach. Those were the times that he had made himself channel Sam, recalling how his uncle had managed to get to him back when he was just like Casey.

It worked, and in the end it had all paid off. That was all he—and Garrett—were ever interested in. The final results. That made everything that had come before— the strategizing, the enduring of endless hostility and curses—all worth it. And he also kept in contact with former "graduates," taking an interest in their lives and making sure that they remained proud of their own progress—and didn't backslide.

So far, he hadn't lost a single teen. He intended to keep it that way.

"Hey, you think that's them?" Garrett asked. Shading his eyes with one hand, he pointed at something behind his brother's back with the other.

Jackson turned around to see a beige, almost nondescript sedan that had definitely seen better days approaching from the north. The road was open, but the driver refrained from speeding, something that tempted a lot of drivers around the area, whether they were tourists or natives.

The closer the vehicle came, the dustier it appeared. Jackson recalled that his new challenge hailed from the state of Indiana. Indianapolis to be precise. And unless the Dallas airport car rental agency was dealing in really beaten-up-looking vehicles these days, his latest boarder had been driven down to Forever rather than coming in by airplane.

Interesting, Jackson thought.

RESTLESS, IMPATIENT AND WORRIED, Ryan Winter shifted in his seat for the umpteenth time even though he had decided more than several hundred miles ago that there was no such thing as a comfortable position in his sister's beat-up, secondhand sedan.

Ryan glared out the window, sulking.

He'd always been able to get his sister to come around to his way of thinking. But the other morning, when she had told him—not asked, but *told*, something he was still angry about—that they were going to a place called Forever, Texas, he'd thought she was kidding. It wasn't until she'd marched into his room and thrown some of his clothes into a suitcase, then grabbed him by the arm and all but thrown *him* into the car after the suitcase, that he realized she was serious.

Dead serious.

He'd tried to reason with her, then he threatened, cajoled and pleaded, going through the entire gamut of ordinarily successful avenues of getting her to change her mind. But every attempt had failed. One by one, his sister had tossed them all by the wayside. She wasn't going to let him talk or con his way out of going to this stupid, smelly horse place, and he was furious.

He'd had all those miles to sufficiently work himself up.

He thought he knew why this was happening. Because he was the reason why her stick-in-the-mud husband had left. But just because her life was falling apart was no reason for her to take it out on him.

Making one last-ditch attempt to get her to turn the car around, Ryan said, "Look, I'm sorry about your marriage breaking up, but the way I see it, I did you a favor. John was a loser, and you're a hell of a lot better off without him. If you're dumping me here at this stupid prison ranch just to get even, it's not going to work because I swear I'm taking off the first chance I get," he added for good measure, thinking that would really get to his sister. Debi was very big on family and he was officially all she had. He felt confident that the threat of losing him would be enough to get his sister to back off about this prison ranch and give him the space he needed. "And if I do leave, you'll never find me."

DEBI'S HANDS TIGHTENED on the steering wheel. It had been a long drive from Indianapolis. She was hot, she was tired and she'd gotten lost half a dozen times during the trip down to this ranch. She fervently hoped this place dealt in miracles on a regular basis because she really, really needed one.

Badly.

Debi had a feeling that nothing short of a miracle was going to save her brother. And maybe even *that* wasn't enough.

She spared her brother a quick glance. He always had a habit of trying to turn things around, of putting her on the defensive. Well, not this time. She couldn't allow it.

"This isn't about my marriage, or lack thereof, this is about you. You're broken, Ryan, and I don't know how to fix you." Even saying it pained her, but it was the truth. Somehow, Ryan had lost his way and she had lost the ability to connect with him. She wasn't too proud to admit that she needed help in both departments.

"Drop-kicking me here to this dude ranch that's built out of horse manure sure as hell isn't going to do it, Debs."

She sincerely hoped that wasn't a prophecy. "I've tried everything else with you and it hasn't worked. Maybe the people who run this ranch will have better luck."

Even as she said it, she mentally crossed her fingers. She'd been at her wits' end and more than desperate the day after she had bailed her brother out of jail. True to his word, John had been gone when she came home with Ryan. The following morning, she'd broken down in the hospital's fifth-floor break room. Trying to comfort her, Sheila, another nurse on the floor, told her about The Healing Ranch.

It turned out that Sheila's cousin had a son who was well on his way to a long rap sheet and possibly life in prison. She had sent him to The Healing Ranch in a last-ditch attempt to save him from himself. According to Sheila, it had worked. Three months later, she'd gotten back the decent kid she'd always known was in there.

Debi had called the number Sheila had given her that very day. She'd had to leave a message on the answering machine, which didn't fill her with much confidence, but that all changed when she received a call back that evening from the man who ran the place. She remembered thinking that Jackson White Eagle had a nice, calming voice. Just talking to him had made her feel that maybe it wasn't really hopeless after all.

He hadn't made her any lofty promises, he'd just said that he would see what could be done and invited her to come down with her brother. Debi hadn't wanted a tour, she'd wanted to sign Ryan up right then and there, afraid that if this Jackson person had a chance to interact with her brother first, he couldn't accept him into the program.

"You're sure you don't want to see the ranch and think about it first?" he had asked her.

Her online research had told her that the man who ran the ranch had a perfect track record so far. That was definitely good enough for her—especially since she had nowhere else to turn.

"I'm sure," she had replied.

She'd taken a leave of absence from the hospital, gotten together what there was in her meager savings account, transferring it into her checking account, and driven down here with Ryan. John's divorce papers were tucked into her purse. She had no one to lean on but herself.

Ryan had put up a huge fuss about being taken away from his friends. He'd also threatened to run away the first chance he got.

He repeated the threat every hour on the hour in case she hadn't heard him the first half a dozen times.

Debi told herself that Ryan only threatened to run away because he wanted to frighten her into turning around and driving back to Indianapolis. Maybe a year ago, she might have, but what stopped her now was that she knew if she did, for all intents and purposes she would have been signing her brother's epitaph because as sure as day followed night, Ryan was on a path headed straight for destruction.

"Well, the clowns who run this place aren't going to get the opportunity to brainwash me because I'm taking off first chance I get. You know I will," he threatened again.

Debi sighed as she stared at the road before her. She wasn't all that sure the threats were empty ones. Ryan could very well mean what he said. That was why she wasn't going back home once she had finished registering him and got him settled in. If Ryan *did* take off, she wanted to be right here where she could go after him and bring him back. He was her brother and at fifteen, obviously still a minor. She was responsible for him, and she would have felt that way even if he were eighteen.

She prayed that it wouldn't come to that, but considering what she had already gone through with Ryan, she wasn't counting on it being easy.

"I mean it. I'm gone. First chance I get," Ryan repeated with emphasis.

"Yes, I heard you," Debi replied stoically. She also heard the fear in his voice. *God, let these people here reach him*, she prayed. She saw the cluster of people in and around the corral. "Okay, we're here. For my sake, try not to insult the man in the first five minutes."

Ryan's laugh had a nasty sound to it, and she knew this was not going to go well. "Hey, I don't want to spoil the man, now, do I?"

She didn't bother answering her brother. Anger and despair had grabbed equal parts of her. Anger that he had allowed himself to become this destructive, negative being and despair because she couldn't snap him out of it and had been forced to turn to strangers for help. She'd thought she was too proud for that but obviously pride had withered and died in the face of this situation.

There were two cowboys by the corral as she pulled up. Were they just workers, or…?

She saw the slightly taller of the two draw away from the enclosure and approach her car. Debi turned off the engine, carefully watching the approaching cowboy's every move. He strolled toward them like a sleek panther, with an economy of steps.

Debi got out of the vehicle. Ryan remained where he was. She wasn't about to leave him in the car, not even if she was only inches away and had the car keys in her hand. She knew her brother, knew that he could hot-wire anything with an engine and take off at a moment's notice. She had no doubt that he probably thought that he could propel himself into the driver's seat and just take off without a single backward glance.

Well, not today, she told herself. Bending down, she looked in through the open window on the driver's side. "Get out of the car, Ryan."

"No," he informed her flatly.

At fifteen, Ryan was taller than she was and while scrawny-looking, he was still stronger. The only time she ever managed to get him to move was when she caught him off guard.

That wasn't going to work here, she realized, looking down into his defiant face.

Jackson White Eagle chose that exact moment to enter into her life. "Trouble, ma'am?"

Chapter Two

"'Ma'am'?" Ryan echoed with a sneer. "Is this guy for real?" he jeered, turning toward his sister.

"Very real," Jackson assured him in an even voice that was devoid of any emotion. "Why don't you get out of the car like your sister requested?" he suggested in the same tone.

"Why don't you mind your own freakin' business?" Ryan retorted, sticking up his chin the way he did whenever he was spoiling for a fight.

"For the next month or two or three," Jackson informed him slowly with emphasis, "you *are* my business, Ryan," he concluded in the same low, evenly controlled voice with which he had greeted the teen's sister.

Jackson opened the door on the passenger side, firmly took hold of Ryan's arm and with one swift, economic movement, pulled his newest "ranch hand," as he liked to call the teens who arrived on his doorstep, out of the car and to his feet.

"Ow!" Ryan cried angrily, grabbing his shoulder as if it had been wrenched out of its socket. "You going to let this jerk manhandle me like that?" he demanded angrily, directing the question at his sister.

Before Debi had a chance to respond, Jackson told her brother matter-of-factly, "That didn't hurt, Ryan."

"How do you know?" Ryan cried, still holding his shoulder as if he expected his arm to drop off.

"Because," Jackson said in a calm, steely voice, "if I had wanted to hurt you, Ryan, trust me, you would have known it. To begin with, the pain would have thrown you off balance and you would have dropped like a stone to your knees." He released his hold on Ryan's arm, but his eyes still held Ryan prisoner. "Now then, why don't you get your things out of the car and come with me? I'll show you and your sister where you'll be staying for the next few months."

"Few months?" Ryan repeated indignantly. "The hell I will."

Jackson suppressed a sigh. He turned from the woman who he was about to escort to the ranch house and looked back at the teen she had brought for him to essentially "fix." This one, he had a feeling, was going to take a bit of concentrated effort.

"By the way," he said to Ryan, "I let the first two occasions slide because you're new here and this is your first day—"

"And my last," Ryan interjected.

Debi had stood by, quiet, until she couldn't endure it any longer. "Ryan!"

The smile Jackson offered to the woman who had brought the teen to him was an understanding one.

"That's all right. Ryan will come around." His eyes shifted to the teen. Under all that bravado was just a scared kid, he thought. A kid he intended to reach—but it wouldn't be easy. "There's a fine for every time you curse. You put a dollar into the swear jar."

"Curse?" Ryan mocked. "You call that a curse?" he asked incredulously.

"Yes, I do. While you're here you're going to have to clean up your language as well as your act," Jackson informed the teen.

Ryan rolled his eyes. "Pay him the damn fine so he'll stop whining," Ryan told his sister.

"That's three now," Jackson corrected quietly. "That one isn't free. And you're the one who needs to pay, not your sister. Time you learned to pull your own weight. Your sister can't be expected to always be cleaning up your messes."

"Yeah, well, a lot you know," Ryan retorted, an underlying frustration in his voice. "My sister's the one with all the money."

"That'll change," Jackson informed him. "You'll be earning your own money while you're here. Everyone at The Healing Ranch earns his own money by doing the chores that are assigned to him. You'll get yours after you settle in."

"Wow," Ryan marveled. "How lame can you get?"

Ryan shifted from foot to foot, eyeing his sister and obviously waiting for her to say something to back him up—or better yet, to spring him so he could stop playing this ridiculous game and go home.

Debi's cheeks began to redden. "I'm sorry about this," she apologized to Jackson.

Jackson waved away the apology. "Don't worry about it. We've had a lot worse here."

"Gee, thanks," Ryan sneered. "You know I'm right here."

"Wouldn't forget it for a second," Jackson assured him.

By then, Garrett had come over to join them. Behind

him, the three teens who were in the corral had stopped working with their horses and were now watching the newest arrival at the ranch try to go up against Jackson. It played out like a minidrama.

Garrett flashed a wide, easy smile at both the newest addition to the crew on the ranch and the young woman who had brought him to them.

"This is my brother, Garrett." Jackson made the introduction to Ryan's worried-looking sister. "We run the ranch together," he added rather needlessly, since the information was also on the website he'd had one of Miss Joan's friends put together for him, Miss Joan being the woman who ran the town's only diner and who was also the town's unofficial matriarch.

Taking the attractive young woman's hand in his, Garrett slipped his other hand over it and shook it. "Welcome to The Healing Ranch, ma'am," he said in all sincerity.

"Who came up with that stupid name, anyway?" Ryan asked. "You?" The last part was directed toward Jackson. "'Cause it sounds like something you'd say," the teen concluded condescendingly.

Garrett treated the question as if it was a legitimate one. He was attempting to defuse the situation. Once upon a time, Jackson had quite a temper, but he now prided himself on keeping that temper completely under wraps.

"Actually," Garrett told Ryan, "it was our uncle. He came up with the name. This was his ranch first," Garrett remembered fondly.

"Oh," Ryan mumbled, looking away. He shoved his hands into his pockets and shrugged, lifting up bony shoulders. "Still a lame name," he muttered not quite under his breath.

Jackson pretended not to hear. "The bunkhouse is right over there," he pointed out.

"Yeah? So what? Why would I want to know where the stupid bunkhouse is?" Ryan asked, the same uncooperative attitude radiating from every word.

"Because that's where you'll be staying," Jackson said. Inwardly, he was braced for a confrontation between the teen and himself.

Ryan's deep brown eyes darkened to an unsettling murky hue. "The hell I am."

"You'd better get to work soon, Ryan. You've already got several fines—and counting—against you," Jackson informed him. "Garrett, why don't you take Ryan here—" he nodded at the teen "—and introduce him to the others?"

"Others?" Ryan repeated. "Is this where you bring out a bunch of robotlike zombies and tell me they're going to be my new best friends and roommates? Thanks, but I'll pass."

"Ryan, apologize right now, do you hear me?" Debi ordered. Her words might as well have been in Japanese for all the impression they made on Ryan. Watching her brother being taken in hand had her looking both relieved and tense.

"Ryan, drop the attitude," Jackson told him. "You'll find it a whole lot easier to get along with everyone if you do."

Ryan drew himself up to his full six-foot-two height. "Maybe I don't want to get along with 'everyone,'" he retorted.

Jackson looked at the teenager, his expression saying that he knew better than Ryan what was good for him.

But for now, he merely shrugged. "Suit yourself," he

told Ryan. Jackson turned toward the distraught-looking young woman he had spoken to on the phone several days ago. He could feel that protective streak that had turned his life around coming out. "Why don't you come with me to the main house and we'll go over a few things?" he suggested.

She looked over her shoulder back to the bunkhouse. Garrett was already herding her brother over to the structure.

"Debi!" Ryan called out. It was clearly a call for help.

It killed her not to answer her brother. Debi worked her lower lip for a second before asking Jackson, "Is he really going to be staying in that barn?" she asked uncertainly.

"It's the bunkhouse," Jackson corrected politely, trying not to make her feel foolish for getting her terms confused. "And back in the day, that was where ranch hands used to live. It's been renovated a couple of times since then. Don't worry, the wind doesn't whistle through the mismatched slates." The corners of his mouth curved slightly. "The bunkhouse also has proper heating in the winter and even air-conditioning for the summer. All the comforts of home," he added.

Apparently, Ryan wasn't the only family member who needed structure and reassurance, Jackson thought. Ryan's sister had all the signs of someone who was very close to the breaking point and was struggling to hold everything together, if only for appearance's sake.

"If home is a bunkhouse," Debi interjected. It obviously seemed incongruous to her.

"A renovated bunkhouse," Jackson reminded her with an indulgent smile. "Don't worry, your brother will be just fine."

Well, if nothing else, Ryan had certainly proven that

he was a survivor, she thought—if only in body. His spirit was another matter entirely. But then, that was why she had brought Ryan here. To "fix" that part of him.

"Right now, I think I'm more worried about you and your brother," she said.

"Why?" Jackson asked, curious. This, he had to admit, was a first, someone bringing him a lost soul to set straight and being worried about the effect of that person on *him*. "Is Ryan violent?" The teen seemed more crafty than violent, but it paid to be safe—just in case.

"Oh, no, nothing like that," Debi was quick to clarify. "Under all that, he's basically a good kid—but I'll be the first to admit that Ryan is more than the average handful."

"If he wasn't," Jackson pointed out as they made their way to the main house, "then he wouldn't be here—and neither would you."

"True," Debi readily agreed—and then she flushed slightly, realizing what the man with her had to think. "I'm sorry if I sound like I'm being overly protective, but I'm the only family that Ryan has left and I don't feel like I've been doing a very good job of raising him lately." She looked over her shoulder again in the direction her brother had gone as he left the area.

She spotted him with Garrett. The two were headed for the bunkhouse. Garrett had one arm around her brother's shoulders—most likely, in her estimation, to keep Ryan from darting off. Not that there was anywhere for him to go, she thought. The ranch was some distance from the stamp-sized town they had driven through.

"He'll be all right," Jackson assured her. "Garrett hasn't lost a ranch hand yet."

"Is that what you call the boys who come here?" she

asked, thinking it wasn't exactly an accurate label for them. After all, they were here to be reformed, not to work on the ranch, right?

She looked at Jackson, waiting for him to clarify things. What he said made her more confused. The man seemed very nice, but nice didn't get things done and besides, "nice" could also be a facade. That was the way it had been with John. And it had fooled her completely.

"I found that 'ranch hand' is rather a neutral title and, when you come right down to it, the boys *do* work on the ranch. My office is right in here," he told her as he opened the door for her.

She was going to ask him more about having the boys work on his ranch—had she just supplied him with two more hands to do his bidding?—but when he opened the door to his ranch house without using a key, her attention was diverted in an entirely different direction.

"Your door's not locked," she said in surprise.

He heard the wonder in her voice and suppressed a smile. He knew exactly what she had to be thinking. "No, it's not."

"Do you think that's wise?" she asked. "I mean, if you and your brother are outside, working, isn't that like waving temptation right in front of the boys that you're trying to reform?"

"They're on the honor system," he explained, closing the door behind her. "I want them to know that we trust them to do the right thing. You have to give trust in order to get it. Around here, the boys keep each other honest. For the most part, the ones who have been here the longest set an example and watch over the ones who came in last."

She looked at him skeptically. "That sounds a little risky."

"We find it works," he told her. "And just for the record, 'I' don't reform them. What we do here is present them with the right set of circumstances so that they can reform themselves. Most of the time I find that if I expect the best from the teens who come here, they eventually try to live up to my expectations."

Debi looked around. The living room she had just walked into was exactly what she would have expected: open and massive, with very masculine-looking leather furniture, creased with age and use. The sofas—there were two—were arranged around a brick fireplace. The ceiling was vaulted with wooden beams running through the length of it. The only concession to the present was the skylight. Without it, she had a feeling that the room would have a dungeonlike atmosphere.

The rustic feel of the decor seem like pure Texas. Debi really had no idea why that would make her feel safe, but it did.

Maybe it had to do with the man beside her. There was something about his manner that gave her hope and made her feel that everything was going to work out.

She knew she wasn't being realistic, but then, she'd never been in this sort of situation before.

Realizing that she'd fallen behind as he was walking through the room, Debi stepped up her pace and caught up to Jackson just as he entered a far more cluttered room that she assumed was his office.

"Sounds good in theory," she acknowledged, referring to his ideas about trust.

"Works in practice, too," he told her with just the tiniest bit of pride evident in his cadence.

Sweeping a number of files, oversized envelopes and a few other miscellaneous things off a chair, Jackson nodded toward it. He deposited the armload of paraphernalia on the nearest flat surface.

"Please, sit," he requested.

Debi did as he asked, perching on the edge of the seat. She appeared as if she was ready to jump to her feet at any given moment for any given reason, he noted.

This woman was wound up as tightly as her brother. Maybe more so. Undoubtedly because she was constantly on her guard and vigilant for the next thing to go wrong. And he had a feeling that she was doing it alone. She'd said she was the teen's only family.

"So," Jackson began as he sat down in his late uncle's overstuffed, black leather chair. It creaked ever so slightly in protest due to its age. To Jackson, the sound was like a greeting from an old friend. "What do you think is Ryan's story?"

Debi blinked, caught completely off guard. His wording confused her. Did he believe she wasn't involved in her brother's life and could only make a wild guess as to why he was the way he was? Her problem was she was *too* involved in her brother's story.

"Excuse me?" she demanded, forgetting all about feeling as if she had failed her brother.

Jackson patiently explained the meaning behind his question. "Every parent or guardian who comes to us usually has some sort of a theory as to why the boy they brought to us is the way he is. They give me a backstory and I take it from there. Sometimes they're right, sometimes they're wrong. Not everything is black or white." He leaned back in the chair. The motion was accom panied by another pronounced creak. "What's Ryan's backstory?"

He *did* think she wasn't involved, Debi thought. She set out to show this man how wrong he was by giving him a summarized version of Ryan's life.

"As a little boy, Ryan was almost perfect," she recalled fondly. "Never talked back, went to school without a single word of protest. Kept his room neat, ate whatever was on his plate. Did his homework and got excellent grades. He was almost *too* good," she added wistfully, wishing fervently for those days to be back again.

No one was ever too good, but he refrained from commenting on that. Instead, Jackson gently urged the woman on. "And then…?"

It took her a moment to begin. Remembering still hurt beyond words. "And then, three years ago, he was involved in a car accident. He was in the car with my parents." A lump formed in her throat, the way it always did. "They were coming out to visit me—I was away at college."

She would forever feel guilty about that. Guilty about selecting her college strictly because that was where John was going. If she'd attended a college close to home, the way her parents had hoped, this wouldn't have happened.

"Except that they never made it," she said after a beat, forcing the words out. "A truck hauling tires or car batteries or something like that sideswiped them." She had no idea why it bothered her that she didn't have all the details down, but it did. "The car went off the side of the road, tumbled twice and when it was over…" Her voice shook as she continued. "My parents were both dead." Taking a breath, she continued, "And Ryan was in ICU. They kept him in the hospital for almost a month. Even when he got out, he had to have physical therapy treatments for the next six months."

Jackson listened quietly. When she paused, he took the opportunity to comment. "Sounds like he had a pretty hard time of it."

Debi took in a long, shaky breath. It hadn't exactly been a walk in the park for her, either. But this wasn't about her, she reminded herself sternly. It was about Ryan. About *saving* Ryan.

"He did," she answered. "He kept asking me why he was the one who got to live and they had to die." A rueful smile touched her lips. "That was while he was still talking to me. But that got to be less and less and then the only time we talked at all was when I was nagging him to do his homework and stop cutting classes." The sigh escaped before she could stop it. "I guess you could say that they were one-way conversations."

He was all too familiar with that—from both sides of the divide, he thought.

"What brought you here to The Healing Ranch?" he asked her. When Debi looked at him, confused, he explained, "It's usually the last straw or the one thing that a parent or guardian just couldn't allow to let slide."

She steeled herself as she began to answer the man's question. "I had to bail Ryan out of jail. He ditched school and was hanging around with a couple of guys I kept telling him to avoid. One of them stole a car." She had a pretty good idea which one had done it, but Ryan refused to confirm her suspicions. "According to what another one of the 'boys' said, the guy claimed he was 'borrowing' it just for a quick joy ride. The owner reported the car missing and the police managed to track it down fairly quickly. The boys were all apprehended."

Age-wise they were still all children to her, not young men on their way to compiling serious criminal records.

"But first they had to chase them through half the city." She didn't want to make excuses for her brother, but she did want Jackson to know the complete truth. "Ryan didn't steal the car, but he knew it didn't belong to the kid behind the wheel. He should have never gotten into the car knowing that." This time, she didn't even bother trying to suppress her sigh or her distress. "He used to make better decisions than that," she told the man sitting opposite her.

A lone tear slid down her cheek. She could feel it and the fact that it was there annoyed Debi to no end. She didn't want to be a stereotypical female, crying because the situation was out of her control. She couldn't, *wouldn't* tolerate any pity.

Using the back of her hand, she wiped away the incriminating stain from her cheek.

"Sorry," she murmured. "I'm just a little tired after that long trip."

Rather than comment on what they both knew was an extremely lightweight excuse, Jackson took the box of tissues he'd kept on his desk and pushed it over toward the young woman.

He watched her pull one out, his attention focused on her hand. Her left hand. There was no ring on her ring finger—but there was a very light tan line indicating that there'd been a ring there not all that long ago.

"Did your marriage break up over that?" he asked her gently.

Debi raised her eyes to his in wonder as she felt the air in her lungs come to a standstill.

How did he know?

Chapter Three

Debi stared at the man sitting across from her. Had Sheila called him to set things up for her? She hadn't mentioned anything, but if her coworker and friend hadn't called this man, then how did Jackson know about the current state, or non-state, of her marriage?

"Excuse me?" she said in a voice filled with disbelief.

Even as he asked the question, Jackson was fairly certain that he already knew the answer. Whoever this woman's husband had been, the man was clearly an idiot. Two minutes into their interview, he could tell that Deborah Kincannon was a kind, caring person. That she seemed to be temporarily in over her head was beside the point. That sort of thing happened to everyone at one point or another. It certainly had to his stepmother.

The fact that Ryan's sister was exceedingly attractive in a sweet, comfortable sort of way wasn't exactly a hardship, either. The more he thought about it, the more convinced he was that her choice in men, or at least in *this* man, left something to be desired.

"Did your marriage break up over that?" he repeated. Jackson could almost hear the way the scene had played out. "Your husband said he'd had enough of your brother's actions and told you to wash your hands of him, am I right?"

Debi could feel herself growing pale. The second this man said the words, she remembered the awful scenario and how it had drained her.

Her mouth felt dry as she asked, "How did you…?" Her voice trailed off as she looked at Jackson incredulously.

"Your ring finger," he answered, nodding at her left hand. "There's a slight tan line around it, like you'd had a ring on there for a while—until just recently."

Debi nodded and looked down at her left ring finger. It still felt strange not to see her wedding ring there. She hadn't taken the ring off since the day she'd gotten married, not even to clean it. She'd found a way to accomplish that while the ring remained on her finger. But now there seemed to be no point in continuing to wear it. If she did, it would not only be perpetuating a lie, it would also remind her that she had wasted all those years of her life, loving a man who was more a fabrication than real flesh and blood.

The John Kincannon she had loved hadn't existed, except perhaps in her mind.

Stupid, stupid, stupid, she couldn't help thinking. There had been signs. Why hadn't she allowed them to register?

She supposed the answer lay in the fact that she just couldn't admit to herself that she could have been so wrong about a person for so many years. A person she had given up so much for. A person who had inadvertently caused her to sacrifice her parents' lives. So when warning signs had raised their heads, she'd ignored them, pretending that they didn't exist. Whenever she found herself stumbling across another warning sign, she'd just pretended that it was a little rough patch and everything was all right. How wrong she'd been.

Debi cleared her throat and sat a little straighter in her seat.

"I don't see how that would matter, one way or another," she finally replied, sounding somewhat removed and formal.

Jackson pretended not to take notice of the shift in her voice and demeanor. "Oh, it does," he assured her. "It does. I'm not trying to pry into your private life. I just want to identify all the pieces that make up your brother's life. If your marriage broke up because of him, then Ryan might have that much more guilt he's carrying around."

The laugh that suddenly left her lips had a sad, hollow sound. "Oh, you don't have to worry about that, Mr., um, White Eagle—"

"Jackson," he corrected.

That felt easier for her. As if they were in this together.

"Jackson," she repeated, then continued with what she wanted to tell him. "If Ryan feels responsible for my marriage falling apart, to him that's a very good thing. He and John never got along and he never really liked him. The feeling, I'm sorry to say, was mutual. If anything, that's the one thing Ryan feels good about," she said ruefully. "Getting John to leave our house."

She seemed very sure of that, Jackson observed, but for his part, he wasn't, not at this point. "You might be surprised."

"Surprised? Mr. Wh— Jackson, I would be completely flabbergasted if this didn't thrill my brother to death," she said, waving her hand dismissively as if literally pushing this subject to the side. There were more pressing things she wanted to get straight. "Exactly how does your program work?" she asked.

Jackson had always favored an economy of words. "Very simply, we put the boys to work."

"In other words, free labor."

"No, not free," he corrected. "They earn a small salary. The exact amount depends on how well they do the job they're assigned."

Everything he was talking about was entirely new to her. "You *grade* their work?"

"Sure," he freely admitted. Seeing that she was having trouble digesting what he was telling her, he decided to try to clarify things for her. "Let me give you an example. If the job is to clean out the horse stalls and he does the bare minimum, his 'pay' reflects that. If, on the other hand, the stall is clean, there's fresh hay put out, fresh water in the trough, that kind of thing, then his pay reflects *that*. It gives them an incentive to work hard and do well. It also teaches them that doing a good job pays off. We want them feeling good about what they accomplish and, by proxy, good about themselves.

"What we're hoping for, long-term, is that the guys get used to always doing their best and trying their hardest."

"Why horses?" she asked.

The question seemed to come out of nowhere.

Jackson smiled, more to himself than at her. His first response was one he didn't voice. He was simply passing on the method that his uncle had used with him. For the most part, though he dealt with tough cases and teens that came with extrawide chips on their shoulder, Jackson was a private person who would have been content just to keep to himself. But after his uncle's death, he'd felt compelled to take his uncle's lessons and methods and put them to use.

Still, that didn't mean baring his own soul—or parts thereof—to someone he really didn't know.

"Easy," he answered. "I work with what I have. Besides, it's been proven that people bond more easily with animals than they do with other people. Having a hand in the care, feeding and grooming of these horses brings order and discipline into the boys' lives. It teaches them patience—eventually," he specified, recalling that the horse Sam had given him to work with had seemed to be every bit as headstrong and difficult to deal with as he was at the time. It had been a battle of wills before he finally emerged victorious.

The greatest day of his life had been when he finally got Wildfire to respond to his key signals. He'd felt high on that for a week. After that, he no longer had any desire to seek out artificial ways of escape—he'd found it in working with Wildfire.

Debi leaned forward, folding her hands before her—making him think of an earnest schoolgirl. "Do you think you can help my brother?"

He didn't answer her immediately. Instead, he had a question of his own first. "Is going along for a joy ride in the car his friend stole the worst thing he's ever done?"

"Yes," she answered with conviction, then realized that she had no right to sound that sure. "To the best of my knowledge," she qualified in a slightly less certain voice.

"Then it's my opinion that Ryan can be turned around," he told her. "Since you're here, I'll need to have you fill out some forms. Nothing unusual, just education level, how many run-ins with the police he's had, how long he's had an attitude problem, any allergies, medical conditions, where we can get in contact with you, that sort of thing," he explained, opening a deep drawer on the right side of his desk.

Digging into it, he found what he was looking for and placed the forms in question on his desk while he shut the drawer.

"To answer your last question, I'll be close by while Ryan's here at the ranch," she told him as she accepted the papers he handed her.

For the most part, guardians asked to be called and then returned home, wherever home happened to be. "Define 'close by,'" he requested.

It was Debi's turn to smile.

Even the slight shift in her lips seemed to bring out a radiance, just for a moment, that hadn't been noticeable before. Jackson caught himself staring and forced himself to look away.

An unsettled feeling in his gut lingered a little longer.

"Don't worry, I'm not going to be parked on some hillside, looking down and watching his—and your— every move if that's what you're worried about," she told Jackson.

"I just thought it might be uncomfortable for you to sleep in your car," he said. She had no idea whether or not he was kidding or serious. It shouldn't matter whether or not she was uncomfortable or not. "If you need a place to stay, Miss Joan is always willing to open her doors and temporarily take someone in."

"Miss Joan?" Debi repeated quizzically. The setup he mentioned sounded suspiciously like a brothel to her. When had she gotten so distrusting? she wondered. It had crept up on her when she hadn't been paying attention.

Jackson nodded. "She runs the local diner and is kind

of like a self-appointed mother hen to the town in general."

There was a fondness in his voice whenever he mentioned the outspoken older woman. Miss Joan had a no-nonsense way of talking and a big heart made out of pure marshmallow. When Sam had taken him under his wing, his uncle and Miss Joan were seeing one another. The relationship continued for a couple of years before they unexpectedly just went their separate ways. At the time, he was curious as to why they had split up, but when he brought the matter up, Sam merely gave him a long, penetrating look and said nothing. Any attempt to get information from Miss Joan went nowhere, as well. Miss Joan wasn't one to talk about herself at all.

Consequently, he'd never found out what had gone wrong, but whenever he did find time to stop by the diner for a cup of coffee, Miss Joan always told him it was on the house, adding that Sam would have disapproved if she charged him for it.

"Why would I stay with her?" Debi asked.

It didn't make any sense to her. After all, the woman didn't know her from Adam—or Eve. If she were in this woman's place, she certainly wouldn't take in a stranger. Things like that just weren't done these days. There was trusting, and then there was being incredibly naive.

She had a feeling that if she said as much to this cowboy, she'd offend him, so she kept her comment to herself. But it didn't change her opinion.

"I thought I saw a sign when I was passing by Forever that said something about a new hotel having a grand opening."

He'd forgotten about that. In his defense, he didn't get to town very often these days and the hotel was practi cally brand-new, having opened its doors less than five months ago. What he recalled was that building the hotel had been a huge shot in the arm for a lot of his friends on the reservation, providing many of them with construction work.

"It's not just a new hotel," he informed her. "It's Forever's *only* hotel, as well."

"You don't have any other hotels in town?" she asked in wonder.

That sounded almost impossible, Debi thought. Indianapolis had over two hundred of them. How could this town have just one—and recently built at that?

Maybe she had made a mistake in bringing Ryan here after all.

What choice did you have? she asked herself. And this wasn't about how big or little the town was. This was about the ranch's track record, which, according to Sheila, as well as the internet, was perfect so far.

"If you'd have come here a year ago, we wouldn't have had this one," Jackson was telling her. "The people in Forever don't exactly believe in rushing into things," he explained with a soft laugh.

Debi was unprepared for the sound to travel right under her skin, but it did, probably because she was vulnerable. Having the man she had once thought of as the love of her life walk out on her had sent her self-esteem crashing to subbasement level. It made her doubt all of her previous assumptions and had her feeling that she couldn't trust her own judgment. Everything that she had believed she'd had turned out to be a lie—why would anything be different from here on in?

"Apparently," she agreed, feeling as if she was moving through some sort of a bad dream—a dream she couldn't wake up from.

She glanced down at the forms he'd just given her and tried to shake off her mood. "Do you want me to fill them out now?" she asked. It might be easier for her to tackle the forms tonight, after she checked in to this new hotel and went to her room.

"If you don't mind, I'd like that, yes," he told her. "I learned that it's better not to put things off," Jackson explained. Rising to give her some breathing room while she filled the forms out, he asked, "Would you like something to drink? Coffee? Tea?"

Or me?

Now where the hell had that come from? Jackson upbraided himself. That had to be something he'd unknowingly picked up from a program that had been playing in the background, or that he'd seen as a kid. When his parents were arguing, he'd turn the TV up loud to block them out so he could pretend that everything was really all right and that they weren't screaming all sorts of terrible things to and about each other.

Jackson looked a little closer at Ryan's sister. There was something almost appealingly vulnerable about her that brought out the protector in him. He was going to have to be careful to keep that under wraps, he warned himself.

Debi stopped perusing the forms and looked up at him, clearly surprised. "You have tea?"

"Yes. We're not entirely barbaric out here in Texas," Jackson told her, amused by her surprised expression.

Realizing that she might have insulted the man, Debi did what she could to backtrack and remove her foot from her mouth.

"I'm sorry, I didn't mean to imply anything. It's just that, well, I can't visualize you actually drinking tea."

"I don't," he told her, then answered the question he knew she was thinking. "I keep tea around for guests. I like being prepared." He paused, waiting. But she didn't comment or make a request. He tried again. "So, can I get you that tea?"

Debi shook her head. "No, that's okay," she answered. "I'm good."

Yes, you are.

There it was again, he thought. Unbidden thoughts popping up in his head. This wasn't like him. Besides, the woman wasn't even his type. Any woman he had ever socialized with either came from the reservation, or had ties to it.

Maybe he'd been spending too much time with the horses in his off hours. Lately, he'd been devoting himself to the boys and the ranch to the exclusion of everything else. Maybe that had taken its toll on him and this was his body's way of getting back at him. It was reminding him that he needed to get out and mingle a little bit with people who didn't come with a list of problems and lives they needed to have turned around.

It was getting to the point that he was forgetting that there were people like that out there. People whose souls *weren't* troubled.

Jackson forced his mind back to the woman who regarded him as if he was her last hope in the world. At this point in time, he probably was.

"We've also got a couple of cans of diet soda and then there's always that old standby, water."

But Debi shook her head to that as she started filling out the forms. "No, really, I'm fine. Nothing to drink for me, thank you," she told him, sparing Jackson a quick glance before looking back at the questionnaire on the desk before her.

"Would you know of anywhere that I could get a job?" she asked.

If she needed a job, that was going to put an entirely different spin on matters, Jackson thought. Most likely, the woman wouldn't be able to afford the down payment for her brother's treatment.

Since he prided himself on never turning away anyone in need, he was going to have to come up with a way to fix that situation.

He approached the subject cautiously. "You're out of work?"

Her head popped up. "What? Oh, no, I have a job waiting for me back home. I just took a leave of absence so that I could be close by if either Ryan or you needed me."

Now that was a loaded sentence that he wasn't about to allow himself to touch with a ten-foot pole, Jackson thought.

"What kind of work do you do?" he asked her. "Because Miss Joan could always give you work at the diner. She's got a lot of part-time waitresses and a good many of them come and go, especially the ones who work at the diner just to get some extra cash that'll supplement their regular income."

"I'm a surgical nurse," she replied. "You wouldn't be hiding a regular hospital out here, would you?" She hadn't seen evidence of one when she'd driven down the town's Main Street, but that didn't mean that there wasn't a hospital around somewhere.

Jackson shook his head. "It's a real pity, but we don't

have one," he confirmed. "The closest hospital to For-ever is in the next town, some fifty miles down the road."

He made it sound as if it was just a hop, skip and a jump away—and it was a little more than that. She sup-posed it was all in how a person viewed things and where they grew up. Compared to where she came from—Indi-anapolis—Forever seemed incredibly tiny. Not only that, but the city had its share of hospitals, as well.

Why would anyone stay in a place like this where their options were so limited? she couldn't help wondering. It was a surprise to her that everyone didn't just pick up and leave town the minute that they graduated high school. She knew she would have. The pace here felt as if it had been dipped in molasses on the coldest day in January.

"We do, however," Jackson told her after a beat, "have a medical clinic, and the doctors there are always look-ing for more help."

A medical clinic. She could work with that. "They might just have found it," she told him with a relieved smile.

Chapter Four

Jackson thought of Daniel Davenport and Alisha Cordell-Murphy, the two doctors who ran the clinic, and the overworked nurse at the desk, Holly Rodriguez. He'd had occasion to interact with all of them at one time or another. Not directly for himself, but he'd brought several of his friends from the reservation in to be treated there.

The clinic was definitely a godsend, seeing as how not all that long ago there hadn't been *any* doctor within fifty miles of Forever.

However, godsend or not, the clinic was woefully understaffed. He wasn't sure if Forever and its surrounding area was growing, or if the doctors had just become overwhelmed and slowed down. But it was clear that help was definitely needed.

The doctors would be thrilled at the mere thought of getting even temporary help for a short respite. He knew that for certain, recalling what Dr. Davenport had said when it had been just him running the clinic with Holly's help, and Dr. Cordell-Murphy—she'd been just Dr. Cordell at the time—had arrived in response to an open recruitment letter he'd sent to his old hospital in New York.

"After you finish filling out the paperwork," Jackson

told the nurse, "I can have one of the boys take you to the clinic."

Debi paused for a moment. "Is it in town?" she asked.

"Yes, ma'am, it is."

She winced at the word he'd used to address her. "Please, don't call me *ma'am*," she requested earnestly. "It makes me feel like I'm at least eighty years old."

"Just a sign of respect, nothing more," he replied. "And just for the record, you'd be the *youngest*-looking eighty-year-old on the planet," Jackson told her with a wink.

Debi felt something in her stomach flutter in response to the wink. Whether the man knew it or not, that was an extremely sexy wink.

Even so, she had no business reacting like that. She told herself that it was just because she hadn't really eaten in more than twenty-four hours.

This decision to drag her brother to a horse ranch almost fifteen hundred miles from home hadn't been an easy one for her. Neither had driving all the way to Forever by herself.

Ryan didn't have a license, but he did, she'd discovered, know how to drive. That changed nothing. There was no way she would have allowed him behind the wheel, despite the volley of curses he'd sent her way. Had she given in—there were exceedingly long, lonely stretches of road with nothing in sight—she had no doubt that he would have driven them to who-knows-where while she caught a few much-needed winks.

So she had loaded up on energy drinks and coffee and driven the entire distance by herself. Fast.

That left her exhausted and yet wired at the same time. The thought of being in the car with someone who had been sent to The Healing Ranch to be reformed made her somewhat uncomfortable. She would have no idea what to expect or what could happen. What if, like Ryan, her would-be guide would use the opportunity to try to escape from Forever and the ranch?

"No need to take up anyone's time," she told Jackson. "I can get to the town on my own. But after we get all this paperwork squared away, I would like to see the bunkhouse, please."

"So you can see for yourself that it's not some primitive dungeon?" Jackson guessed, deliberately exaggerating what she probably assumed about the conditions in the bunkhouse.

Debi opened her mouth, then decided there was no point in trying to deny what he seemed to have already figured out. "Yes."

Her admission surprised him a little. But it also pleased him. She was brave enough not to try to divert or dress up the truth.

"Sounds to me like Ryan has a good role model to look up to once we get him straightened out and back to tapping into his full potential," Jackson observed.

"I don't know about that," she said as she continued filling in the forms. "If I'm such a good role model, why did he get to the point that I had to bring him somewhere like this or risk losing him altogether?"

Jackson had been doing this for a while now and it never ceased to amaze him how many different reasons there were for teens to act out. "It's not always clear to us," he told her. "Sometimes it takes a while to understand."

"So," Debi observed wryly, "you're a philosopher as well as a cowboy."

"A man wears a lot of hats in his lifetime," was Jackson's only reply.

Working as quickly as she was able, Debi filled out all the forms and signed her name on the bottom of the last one. After she was finished, she gathered all the pages together, placing them in a small, neat pile. She felt exhausted and was running pretty close to empty, but the espresso coffee she had saved for last on her trip here was giving her a final shot in the arm.

Pushing the pile of forms to one side, Debi took out her checkbook. Funds were growing dangerously low, thanks to John and the divorce he seemed to have processed at lightning speed. Bringing Ryan here was probably going to eat up every spare dime she had. That was one of the reasons she'd driven here instead of flying.

"I assume you prefer being paid up front." Turning to the next blank check, Debi asked, "What should I make it out for?"

If the woman was taking a leave of absence to be near her brother while he was here and if she was looking for employment, that meant she was probably living close to hand to mouth.

Jackson placed his hand over her checkbook, stopping her from beginning to date the check. "Why don't you hold off on that until he's been here a week?"

"Why? Because you might decide he's incorrigible and you'll hand him back to me? Won't you still want to get paid for 'time served' if that's the case?"

"Actually, I was thinking about you," Jackson said simply. "I figured that you might decide you're not happy with the program we have here and want to take your brother home."

She flushed, embarrassed for the conclusion she'd leaped to. Lately, she'd been too edgy, too quick to take offense where none was intended.

"I'm sorry, I didn't used to be this way," she apologized. "The last six months have taken a toll on…on all of us," she said, changing direction at the last minute. She'd meant to say that the past six months had taken a toll on her, but that sounded terribly selfish and self-centered to her own ear—even though arguing with John over Ryan had completely worn her down to a nub.

"All?" Jackson questioned, his tone coaxing more information out of her.

Debi obliged without even realizing it at first. "On Ryan, and me—and John." She saw the unspoken question in Jackson's eyes. "John is my ex."

"Oh." The single word seemed to speak volumes— and yet, how could it? she thought. Maybe she was just getting punchy.

She avoided Jackson's eyes and got back to her initial apology. "I apologize if I sound abrupt."

"No apologies necessary," Jackson told her, carelessly waving her words away like so much swirling dust. "I've heard and seen a lot worse than anything you might think you're guilty of."

Every time he dealt with the parents or guardians of one of the teens brought or sent to his ranch, it reminded him just what he had to have put his stepmother through. The woman had been nothing but fair and good to him when she didn't have to be, taking him in after his father had taken off. Heaven knew his own father never felt anything for him, neither affection nor a sense of responsibility.

Yet somehow Sylvia had, and in return he had treated her shamefully, putting her through hell before he finally was forced to get his act together, which he did, thanks to Sam.

She was gone now, but remembering her made him more considerate of the people who brought their troubled teens to him to be, in effect, "fixed."

"Okay, everything looks in order," he told Ryan's sister, glancing through the forms quickly. "Let me take you on that tour of the bunkhouse to set your mind at ease," he offered.

"I'd like that," she told him. She wanted to see the bunkhouse and felt that since he was the one in charge of the ranch and its program, he would be the best one to conduct the tour.

And if something turned out to be wrong in her eyes, he was the one to be held accountable.

Debi got up and immediately paled. She'd risen a little too quickly from her seat. As a result, she immediately felt a little light-headed and dizzy. Trying to anchor herself down, she swayed ever so slightly. Panicked, she made a grab for the first thing her hand came in contact with to steady herself.

It turned out to be the cowboy standing next to her.

Jackson seemed to react automatically. His free arm went around her, holding her in place. Thanks to capricious logistics, that place turned out to be against his chest.

The light-headedness left as quickly as it had appeared. The air in her lungs went along with it as it whooshed out the second she found herself all but flush against the cowboy's chest and torso.

Their eyes met and held for an eternal second—and then Jackson loosened his hold on her as he asked, "Are you all right?"

Yes!

No!

I don't know.

All three responses took a turn flashing through her brain as the rest of her tried to figure out just what had happened here.

Bit by bit, what transpired—and why—came back to her in tiny flashes. "Sorry, I got a little dizzy," she apologized. Dropping her line of vision back to the floor, she murmured, "I think I got up too fast." Looking at the arm she had grabbed, she realized that she must have dug her nails into his forearm. There were four deep crescents in his skin. "Oh, God, I'm sorry." She didn't need confirmation that she had done that. She knew.

"No harm done," he told her good-naturedly. Jackson took a step back from her slowly, watching her for any signs that she was going to faint. "We can stay here a little longer if you like."

"No, that's all right. I'd like to see the bunkhouse before your…ranch hands come back to use it."

The bunkhouse, for the most part, was used for sleeping and winding down in the evening after a particularly long, hard day filled with chores.

"The day's still young," he replied. "We have plenty of time." As he spoke, he studied her more closely. She looked exhausted, as well as a little disconnected. "Did you drive here?" he asked.

She started to nod and discovered that made the world spin again, so she stopped immediately.

"Yes."

"From Indianapolis?" He wanted to make sure that he had her starting point down correctly.

"Yes." Her eyebrows drew together in a quizzical expression. "Why?"

Jackson did a quick calculation. "That's roughly fourteen to fifteen hundred miles away," he estimated, impressing her. "How long did that take you?"

Debi had no idea why he was asking her this, but she saw no harm in answering. "A little more than twenty-four hours."

The "why?" was silent, but implied.

That meant she had to have driven straight through to get here that fast. "You were the only one driving?" He didn't expect her to say no—and she didn't.

"Yes, I was the only driver." If she didn't get moving soon, she was going to stretch out on top of his desk, clutter and all, she thought, feeling drained beyond belief.

"Why didn't you stop somewhere for a break—or to spend the night?" he asked.

"I like to drive—and besides, I wasn't tired at the time," she said, deciding not to tell him that she'd been wired for nearly half the trip, determined to get there before exhaustion caught up to her because she was afraid that Ryan would take off and disappear the second she stopped driving.

"When did you last eat?" he asked her, curious.

She'd found a tiny box of really old raisins at the back of her glove compartment. "Do raisins count?"

"Only if they're embedded in an apple crisp pie." His

own main flaw, the way Jackson saw it, was his weakness for all things sweet or bad for him.

No wonder the woman looked like a wraith in the making. She hadn't had any food in a day and probably didn't eat all that well before that. Worry did that to a person, he thought, remembering his stepmother.

"Why don't you come with me to the kitchen and we'll see what I can rustle up?" he suggested.

After standing for a bit, she felt steadier and definitely ready to walk wherever he wanted her to go. "I thought ranchers were against rustling," she said, tongue in cheek.

He pretended to take her seriously for a second. "Interesting. Hungry to the point of light-headedness and you still have a sense of humor. That bodes well as far as survival goes," he commented. "Did Ryan go without eating, too?"

Ryan had always been her first priority, now more than ever. He had to be saved. "I packed a couple of sandwiches and some fruit for him and we went through a couple of drive-throughs. He didn't want to eat." Her brother referred to it as "that junk." As for her, she'd had no appetite. "But he changed his mind when he got hungry."

"Why sandwiches just for Ryan and not you?" Jackson asked, trying to glean as much information as he could about the family dynamics of this newest "ranch hand" he was acquiring.

"I didn't have enough cold cuts available for any sandwiches for me. I just took it for granted that Ryan was going to need his strength when he got here. I could always eat later."

"Lucky for you, this is your 'later,'" Jackson told her.

And then he asked, "How long have you been Ryan's sole guardian?"

"Not sole," she protested. "John and I were both his guardians." At least, that was how she had tried to set things up.

It wasn't hard for Jackson to read between the lines. "And how often did your ex participate in anything that had to do with Ryan?"

"Often," Debi answered automatically as well as defensively. And then she flagged just a little when Jackson continued looking at her as if he was waiting her out. "Okay, not all that much…" Debi admitted reluctantly.

He had a better assessment of the situation. "How about not at all?"

Debi blew out a frustrated breath. "Do you do that a lot?" she asked. When he raised an eyebrow in response to her question, she went on to elaborate. "Just stare at people until you make them squirm mentally?"

The corners of his mouth curved just a hint at her observation. "I find it works pretty well on occasion, although," he recalled, "it never really had an effect on Garrett."

"By the way, you're right," Debi admitted out of the blue.

He stopped just short of the kitchen's threshold to turn around and look at her. The woman had lost him. Right about what? "About Garrett?" he asked.

"No," she shook her head. "About my ex. I made a lot of excuses for him in my head, including that he didn't say anything because he felt he didn't have the right to butt in between Ryan and me. But the truth of it was, he resented the fact that Ryan was living with us and that we—meaning me—were responsible for him financially, emotionally and, well, basically in every way."

Jackson took it all in. "And Ryan picked up on John's resentment." It wasn't a question. He knew how these teens acted and reacted because they were him fifteen years ago.

"I tried my best to shield him, to tell him that John cared, but had a hard time showing it—after all, men are like that," she told Jackson with an air of firm conviction.

"In general, yes," Jackson allowed. "But it's not a hard and fast rule around here. And there are a lot of ways for someone to demonstrate that they care without being blatant about it."

"Maybe," she agreed, only half-ready to concede that there might be some truth in what he was saying. "But John didn't." She was about to say something about the ultimatum her ex had given her, then decided that it was far too personal to share with a person she hardly knew. And besides, even though it was to be shared as a secret, secrets had a way of leaking out when you least expected them to. And she didn't want any of what she had just said to accidentally get back to Ryan. He needed to be protected and sheltered from hurtful things like that. If Jackson knew, he just might let it slip to her brother without even thinking. And that would be terrible.

"Sit." Jackson gestured in the general direction of the long, rectangular table where they took all their meals. There were ten chairs in all. Four on either side of the sturdy, scarred wooden table and one placed at either end. She guessed that the two end chairs were for Jackson and his brother and the others were intended for the teens they had staying on the ranch.

Eight. That many? She thought that Ryan might get lost in the shuffle.

"I'm taking you away from your work," Debi protested even as she complied with his invitation.

"It's all part of a whole," Jackson assured her in an easy tone. "We've got some hash browns and bacon left over from breakfast. I can make you some fresh eggs to go with that," he offered.

She really didn't want to cause any trouble—or work. She went for the leftovers—with one exception. "Bacon and hash browns will be fine. And a cup of coffee—if you have creamer."

Jackson acquiesced easily. "Garrett likes his coffee diluted so you're in luck. We have creamer."

Moving like a skilled short-order cook, Jackson put together a plate of food and had the coffee ready for her in a matter of a few minutes.

"Looks good," she commented. And then a thought hit her. "Won't your cook mind that you're giving away the food?"

"I'm the one who pays for the food, and besides, we don't have a cook," Jackson told Ryan's sister, sliding into the chair directly opposite hers rather than taking a seat at the head of the table. "We all take turns making meals."

"The boys, too?" she asked incredulously.

He saw no reason for her to look that surprised. After all, there were male chefs, damn good ones from what he'd heard. Not that anyone here was in danger of reaching that lofty level. Still, they hadn't poisoned anyone, either, so that was pretty good.

"Absolutely. It's all part of learning how to take care of themselves."

She was still exhausted, still wired, but nonetheless,

she felt a peacefulness tiptoeing forward. Jackson White Eagle sounded like a down-to-earth person. More importantly, he struck her as someone who could handle Ryan.

For the first time since she'd set the wheels in motion, Debi felt confident that she'd made the right choice coming here—no matter what the financial cost would ultimately wind up being for her.

Chapter Five

"That was very good."

Pushing her empty plate off to one side of the table, Debi set down her coffee mug after finishing off her second serving of coffee. She'd been prepared to be polite about Jackson's cooking efforts. What she hadn't been prepared for was that his efforts would actually turn out a meal that wasn't just passable, but really good.

Jackson's broad shoulders rose and fell in a quick, dismissive shrug.

"You were hungry," he pointed out modestly. "Most likely anything outside of three-day-old dirt would have tasted good to you."

Debi made a face at the thought of consuming something like that.

"I know it's not considered polite to contradict my host in his own home, but I wasn't too hungry to tell the difference between good and oh-my-God-what-have-I-just-eaten?" Debi assured him with enthusiasm. The more she thought about it, the more genuinely surprised she was by how good the man's cooking actually was. "Where did you learn how to cook like that? From your mother?" she guessed.

Your mother.

Jackson thought of the woman who'd never had time for him. The woman who had walked out on him and never once, in all these years, tried to get back in contact with him or reconnect in any way.

He shook his head and instead said, "Necessity really is the mother of invention."

Her dealings with Ryan and his recent penchant for secrecy and lies had taught her rather quickly to learn to read between the lines.

"Does that mean you were on your own a lot?" Debi asked.

Jackson knew, because of the nature of the ranch he ran, that he should be used to fielding questions. All sorts of questions. But the side of him that was left to deal with those questions was at war with the private side of him, the side that didn't want people knowing the details of his life—any of the details—because hearing them might just make them feel sorry for him.

There was nothing he welcomed less than pity.

For now, Jackson's answer was a vague "Something like that," hoping that would be the end of it.

Debi glanced over toward the kitchen. "Well, it does show a great deal of initiative. Most guys living on their own would have found a woman to cook for them."

That was what John had done. In John's case, he had found her. Debi couldn't remember a single time when John had offered to prepare something rather than leaving it all up to her. John's idea of serving a meal was opening a pizza box.

Just the smallest hint of a smile passed over Jackson's lips. "I would have wound up starving to death," he told her. "I'm pretty fussy—about everything," he added.

With his looks, she caught herself thinking, Jackson

White Eagle could well afford to be fussy. Women would probably fight with frying pans at ten paces for the right to feed him.

"It was just easier learning how to cook on my own," he told her. "So," he concluded, "you still want that tour of the bunkhouse?"

She struck him as a newly lit rocket that was dying to achieve liftoff. Hard to believe she'd seemed so out of it just a short while ago. She'd been attractive before, and now she was even more so, plus exceedingly sensual.

"Now that you've replenished my energy, I'm ready for that tour more than ever," she replied.

So saying, Debi rose from the table carrying her empty plate and coffee mug in her hands. Jackson watched her as she crossed to the sink and turned on the water. Following behind her, he leaned over and decisively shut off the faucet.

When she looked at him quizzically, he told her, "I'll have one of the hands take care of that."

"I don't mind," she responded in all sincerity.

"But I do," he countered. "The hands are here to learn the benefits of work. Cleaning up after a guest is all part of it. Ready?" he asked her again.

Since there was nothing left for her to do there, Debi quickly dried her hands and nodded. "Ready."

Jackson led the way outside. When he walked right past his truck, which was parked outside the front of the house, and kept on going, she was rather surprised. Back in Indianapolis, any distance that amounted to more than a few steps was traversed using a car. Walking was viewed as a pastime, as in taking a walk around the block. Anything other than that necessitated the use of a vehicle.

But apparently not here.

Not only that, but she discovered that in order to keep up with Jackson, she had to either lengthen her stride or break into a trot. She wound up doing a little of both.

When he realized that he was outpacing her, Jackson deliberately slowed down so that she could wind up walking beside him.

"Why didn't you say anything?" he asked as he fell back to join her.

"You mean like 'why are we galloping?'" Debi asked, amused. "It didn't seem polite."

He waved away her assessment of the situation. "I'm used to going everywhere on my own—occasionally with Garrett. Since he's the same height as I am, he tends to walk as fast as I do," he explained, then apologized. "Sorry, I didn't mean to make you trot."

Really good-looking, polite and he could cook. The man was almost too good to be true—which meant that this was probably just his public facade, Debi decided. No man was too good to be true. She knew that now.

She shrugged off his apology. "No harm done," she responded. "I think of it as burning off calories," Debi added. Whenever possible, she tried to look at things in a positive light. It was a coping mechanism that she employed.

Her last comment had him looking at her, his gaze lingering longer than he'd intended because he was verifying something for himself. "Why would you want to burn off calories?"

"Same reason every woman would, to noticeably slim down."

The way the female mind worked was nothing short of mysterious to him, Jackson concluded. "You slim down 'noticeably,' you'll have to be on the lookout for people wanting to run a flag up along your body." He paused for a moment right before the bunkhouse. "If something is already good, you don't mess with it," he told her matter-of-factly.

"Was that a compliment?" Debi asked, rather stunned if it was. He didn't strike her as someone who bothered with flattery, yet what else could it be?

"'That' was a bunch of words, signifying a thought and forming a conclusion," he answered. "If you feel it was a compliment, then fine, it was a compliment. But it wasn't intended as one. Make of it what you will."

And what do I make of you, Jackson White Eagle? she wondered. No immediate answer came to her.

Moving on, Jackson pushed open the door to the bunkhouse.

"This is it," he told her, acting as a guide. "This is where the hands on the ranch sleep and where they unwind at night after dinner."

Debi looked around slowly. She had walked into a very large communal room. Rather than the bunk beds she'd expected to see, there were two rows of equally spaced twins beds facing one another. Four on one side, four on the other.

Now that she thought about it, she hadn't recalled seeing that many teenage boys on the grounds, but they could very well have been within one of the buildings she'd noted as she'd driven onto the ranch.

Curious, she asked, "How many hands are there currently on the ranch?"

"If you'd asked me that question at the beginning of the month, I would have said we were full up with twelve." They'd had to bring in extra beds at the time, making it more crowded. "But since then I've had a few of them graduate and go back to their homes." It was easy to see that he was quietly proud of that accomplishment. "Currently, counting your brother, we have eight."

She moved about the room slowly, trying to get a feel, a vibration from the area. She would've said that no teens slept in the bunkhouse these days. The neat way the beds were all made was nothing short of impressive. "How many repeaters do you get?"

His eyebrows came together in almost a huddle as he looked at her, puzzled. "Excuse me?"

"How many of the 'hands'—" that word still felt very awkward in her mouth "—that graduate from here fall back into their old habits and wind up coming back to your ranch?"

He didn't have to think. Jackson's answer was immediate. "None."

He seemed pretty positive. "Is that because their parents take them elsewhere?" she asked bluntly. Being blunt had never been her way nor had she found it acceptable, but the situation Ryan had put her in had changed all that.

"No, it's because none of the boys who graduate from here wind up being repeat offenders. They wind up going on to finish high school and they either take up a trade or, in some cases, go on to college." He saw the doubt in her eyes. It was to be expected. He would have been suspicious if she'd been too trusting. "I've got letters from former ranch hands, catching me up on their lives, if you'd like to look them over."

The fact that he had volunteered the letters put a different sort of light on the matter. Jackson didn't know her and thus had no way of knowing whether or not she would take him up on his offer. Bluffing would have been a mistake. The cowboy didn't seem like the type to make mistakes.

She supposed she could say yes and see if that made him uncomfortable, but she already had a strong feeling that it wouldn't. The man struck her as being more than able to hold his own in a war of nerves.

Her gut told her that he wasn't a liar.

"No," she told him simply. "I'll take your word for it."

He nodded as he watched her roam about the room. "Suit yourself, but the letters are available if you ever want to, say, satisfy your curiosity—or put your mind at ease."

She looked around one last time before making her way over to what was a very large bathroom. The door was open so she assumed it wasn't occupied. Peering in, she saw that it had a number of shower stalls, a long counter with five sinks and the same number of bathroom stalls. Closer scrutiny showed that the entire area appeared to be clean enough to eat off. Just like the rest of the bunkhouse.

She found it almost unbelievable.

"Are you sure you have the hands *sleeping* in here?" she asked incredulously. This place was every bit as clean as her own apartment—perhaps even more so.

"Very sure," he answered. Then, to lighten the mood just a bit, he added faux-solemnly, "It's either that, or somebody has substituted some very lifelike robots for the guys who bed down here every night."

With nothing left to see within the bunkhouse, they walked back outside. Jackson pulled the door closed behind him. "Would you like to see the stables, as well?" he suggested.

It was as if Jackson had been expecting her scrutiny,

or at least scrutiny by someone conducting a close re-
view of the premises, but if the ranch was normally in a
state of chaos, there would have been no way to make it
this presentable in a few hours. This had to be the normal
state of affairs on The Healing Ranch, and that alone all
but left her speechless.

"The hay's probably been scrubbed clean," Debi
guessed.

Jackson shook his head. "Too time-consuming," he
deadpanned. And then he added seriously, "I just have
whoever's in charge of the stables that day replace the
old hay with new hay. It's a lot simpler—and cleaner—
that way."

What did she have to lose? It wasn't as if she actually
had a job interview waiting for her. Besides, she did like
horses, even though the closest she'd ever been to one was
in her living room, watching a Western on the TV screen.

"Okay, sure, I'll have a look," she told Jackson gamely.

As it turned out, the stables were close to the bunkhouse. All part of the so-called "hands" bonding process with the horses they were assigned to care for, Debi
surmised.

When she arrived, the doors to the stables were standing wide-open the way, Jackson told her, they were every
day during normal operating hours.

Since they had passed a number of hands working with
horses in the corral, Debi expected to find the stables as
empty as the bunkhouse had been.

But they weren't.

While there were no horses to be seen—they were
all out in the corral—the same wasn't true of the people
Jackson was working with. Specifically, the person ho

was going to work with that day after he finished being her guide on the ranch.

Debi was stunned when she realized that the person dressed in jeans, boots and a plaid shirt, and manning a pitchfork as if he was trying to figure out how he was supposed to handle an oversize dinner fork, was her brother.

She'd overlooked him at first.

An involuntary little gasp of surprise passed her lips and had Ryan looking up. There was nothing but blatant hostility and anger blazing in his eyes when he realized that the sound had come from his sister and that she was here, looking at him.

"You come here to gloat?" Ryan demanded nastily. "Or maybe you just came by to tell me that this enforced slavery is for my own good."

"It's not 'slavery' and it is for your own good, Ryan," she said, feeling helpless and taken advantage of as well as angry at her brother's tone.

She'd put up with so much for so long that she was dangerously close to her breaking point. She was seriously worried that she would wind up breaking at the wrong time.

Ryan's eyes narrowed into small, angry, accusing slits. "Well, if it's so damn great, why aren't you in here, shoveling all this sh—"

"Careful, Ryan," Jackson warned, intervening. "You don't want to owe the swear jar more money than you're going to earn this week. If you do, you're going to find that what you ultimately wind up doing will be a whole lot worse than just mucking out the stables."

It wasn't a threat, but a promise. One that was vague enough to mean nothing—or everything. But Jackson

White Eagle did not look like a man to be antagonized without consequences.

Slightly intimidated, Ryan obviously bit back the insult he was about to hurl at both his sister, the betrayer, and the man she had sold him out to.

Ryan changed the wording, but not the tune. "I'm not staying here," he shouted to his sister as she was being escorted away by Jackson. Ryan thought of him as the dark soul who ran this place. "Just giving you fair warning," Ryan shouted even louder. "First chance I get, I'm outta here. I'm gone."

Debi turned and looked over her shoulder at her brother.

"Ryan, please, let them help you," she begged, afraid that her brother would carry out his threat. Afraid that he would wind up dead in some alley before the year was out.

"I don't need their help. I don't need yours, either," Ryan retorted with a nasty edge to his voice.

Each word just cut straight into her heart. There had been a time when they had been close, when she had known or sensed her younger brother's every thought, every need. Now she hardly recognized the angry being he had become.

"Ryan—" she began in a supplicating tone.

The next second, before she could find the words to even remotely try to convince Ryan that being here was a good thing, she felt Jackson taking her arm and leading her away from the stables.

"What are you doing?" she demanded, shaking off his hold.

Jackson released her only once they were outside and several lengths away from the stables.

"The longer you stay in there with him, the more he's going to rant and work himself up," Jackson told her mildly.

She gazed up at him, her concerns piquing. She only heard one thing. "You're telling me I can't talk to my brother?"

"I'm telling you that you can't talk to your brother *now*," he corrected in a voice that was almost maddeningly calm. "Give me a chance to work with him, to show him the right path and make Ryan come around on his own accord."

She was trying very hard to have faith in the process and in the man she was talking to. But in light of her brother's present attitude, it was very difficult for her. "You mean like finding God?"

"God doesn't have to be found. He's not lost," Jackson replied in a voice so mild she found it both soothing and maddening at the same time. "What Ryan has to find is Ryan. He has to stop feeling angry and guilty and all those other hostile emotions that are getting in the way of his own inner growth and evolution. We get him down to the very basics," he explained to Debi, "and then start rebuilding him into a person both you and he can be proud of."

She was beginning to doubt that was even remotely doable. "Sounds like a dream right now," she confessed.

Jackson smiled at her. "Then I guess I'm in the business of making dreams come true," he said before redirecting the conversation. "If there's nothing else that you want to see here, I'll drive you into town." Jackson began leading the way to his vehicle.

That wasn't what the rancher-slash-miracle-worker

had told her earlier. "I thought you said you'd have one of the hands take me."

"I did, but you turned that down, saying you could find the town yourself," he reminded her.

And nothing had changed since then as far as she was concerned. "I still can."

"I have no doubt," Jackson was quick to affirm. "But the way I see it, things'll go faster for you if I introduce you to Doc Davenport myself. Otherwise, you might have to sit out in the waiting room and wait your turn. I don't really recommend that," he added, specifying in a lower voice, "They're *always* busy."

She didn't want to be in his debt, but then, if the man actually managed to turn Ryan around and get him even marginally back to where he had been before things began falling apart, she knew that she would be *eternally* in Jackson's debt until the day she died.

This was a small deal in comparison to that.

"Then I guess," she told him, "you've made me an offer that I can't possibly refuse."

Jackson had no idea that she was paraphrasing a famous movie line. He took it seriously at its face value. "Not wisely, no," he agreed.

"Well, then I won't refuse it," she told him.

Chapter Six

As far as the size of towns went, Forever was more of a whisper rather than a long-winded speech.

While it was true that when it came to Forever's citizens, not everyone knew everyone else, it was a town where everyone at least knew *of* everyone else by name if not by association or sight. However, when it came to those necessary to keeping the town running smoothly and without mishaps, they became known to everyone. People like the town vet, the town doctors, and the store owners since their numbers were few, as well.

The sheriff and his three deputies were familiar faces to one and all even though Forever's worst offenders were a couple of men who preferred spending their time at Murphy's, the town's tavern, to coming home to their sharp-tongued, overbearing wives.

The one person that everyone knew without question was Miss Joan.

Miss Joan had owned and run the local diner for as far back as anyone in town could remember. The diner was the one place where everyone eventually came to meet as well as eat, either on a regular basis or once in a while. Because of this, and the fact that Miss Joan liked to stay on top of everything that was happening in Forever, be it eventful or of no consequence whatsoever, Jackson decided to bring the woman sitting in the passenger side of his truck to the diner first.

And to Miss Joan.

Debi was under the impression that the cowboy was taking her straight to the clinic. So when Jackson pulled up in front of what looked like a diner, the sunshine gleaming off its silver exterior like a lighthouse beacon, she was mildly curious. For a moment, she assumed that he was going to pass by the eatery—cutting it admittedly rather close.

But then he parked.

Debi was growing increasingly aware that the people in this area seemed to march to an entirely different drummer than she was accustomed to, but she just couldn't reconcile herself to the fact that the medical clinic was being run out of a diner.

But he was parking here, and this place was really different from anything she was familiar with back home.

The best way to find out, she decided, was just to ask.

"We're stopping?" She put the question to Jackson as he turned off the ignition and pocketed the key.

"Sure looks that way," he replied, an easy, laid-back drawl curling itself around each word.

Jackson couldn't readily explain why, but the way she seemed to be puzzled by the simplest things amused him—in a good way.

Still, he knew enough about women to know that they didn't like being the source of someone else's amusement, so he kept his reaction to himself. It was undoubtedly safer that way.

Getting out of the cab of his truck, Jackson rounded the hood and came over to her side. He saw that she hadn't opened the passenger door yet, so he opened it for her.

She appeared to be looking at the diner uncertainly.

"The doctors practice out of a diner?" Debi asked incredulously.

He thought of the time that Lady Doc, Alisha—the newest addition to the medical clinic—had treated Nathan McLane, the saloon's best customer, for a ruptured appendix. She'd examined the man on the floor of Murphy's, where he had collapsed.

"The docs practice wherever they're needed," he responded vaguely.

Jackson knew he should have set the record straight immediately as to why he'd stopped here, but he had a feeling that if he said, right off the bat, that he was bringing her here so that Miss Joan could meet her, Ryan's sister would balk at that. Not that there would be any harm done. He'd tell Debi soon enough.

Debi got out of the truck, but then remained where she stood, staring at the gleaming silver structure. "Are you telling me that the clinic is actually located inside a diner?"

"No, but I thought you might want to get a feel for the people in Forever before you offer your services to the docs. This way, you'll have an idea of what you're getting yourself into."

Was he warning her? Or trying to scare her off? She couldn't quite make up her mind about that.

"You make it sound like I'll be making a deal with the devil instead of just making a temporary arrangement to work." That was all she was after, something temporary, just until Ryan was ready to go home. Hopefully, it wouldn't be any longer than a month, tops.

"Oh, no, not with the devil," Jackson assured her. "But being part of Forever—even temporarily—takes commitment and hard work."

Did he think she wasn't up to that? She'd worked hard for every single thing she'd ever gotten. "I'm not a stranger to hard work," she informed him with a touch of indignation.

"Good to hear that," he said so casually, she wondered if he had heard her at all and was merely paying lip service. "C'mon," he went on, "I want to introduce you to someone."

Going up the two steps to the diner, he pulled open the door and held it for her.

Well, at least they didn't lack manners here, she thought.

The second she walked in, the noise level in the partially filled diner—it wasn't lunchtime yet—began to abate until, thirty seconds into her entrance, the noise factor went down to zero.

People seated at the counter as well as in the booths lining the windows turned to look at her.

The red-haired older woman behind the counter paused as she was setting down someone's order. For a split second, the customer appeared to be forgotten.

Sharp hazel eyes swiftly took in the length and breadth of the stranger.

"You brought me a new face, Jackson," the woman said, raising her gravelly voice in order to be heard across the diner.

Debi felt as if she was on display, but her instincts told her that there was no getting around this, not if she intended to remain in this small, backwater town for the duration of Ryan's stay.

And she did.

Debi found the thought of going back home to her empty apartment completely soul draining. Without anyone to talk to there, she would have nothing to do once she got back but dwell on her failed marriage and her failed efforts at raising her very troubled younger brother. Not exactly a heartening scenario.

And what if something went wrong on the ranch while Ryan was there?

Or what if Ryan ran away?

The thought of being almost fifteen hundred miles away at a time like that and being unable to immediately get involved in the search to find him and bring him back to the ranch was something she refused even to contemplate. It was completely unacceptable to her.

She had no choice but to remain in Forever. And if she was to remain here for the duration—however long that might be—then she needed to be able to earn a living. And that meant that she was going to be interacting with the citizens of this collar button of a town. Withdrawing into her shell was not an option that was open to her no matter how enticing it might be.

The woman with the bright orange hair beckoned to her.

"C'mon closer, darlin', I don't bite," the woman promised.

"Don't you believe it," someone within the diner piped up, then laughed at his own statement.

"Don't listen to him, honey. He's just sore because I made him finally pay up his tab." Hazel eyes drew in closer as Miss Joan continued to scrutinize the young woman with Jackson. "So, you passing through or staying?" she asked.

"A little of both," Jackson volunteered before Debi could say anything.

Miss Joan looked at him.

"What's the matter?" she asked Jackson sharply. It was a tone of voice almost everyone in Forever was familiar with. "The girl can't speak for herself?"

Debi straightened her shoulders as her eyes met Miss Joan's. "Of course I can speak for myself," she replied with just a trace of defensiveness.

The next moment, she upbraided herself for her lack of discipline. She was the outsider in this town. If she hoped to fit in, at least marginally, she was going to have to watch that.

Belatedly, Debi offered the woman behind the counter a shy smile.

"So you can." Miss Joan nodded her approval. "What's your name, girl?"

"Deborah Kincannon," Debi answered.

Again, the woman nodded in response. "I expect you already know who I am. So, Deborah Kincannon, what brings you to our town?" When the young woman didn't answer her immediately, Miss Joan glanced over at Jackson. "Guess it's your turn to play ventriloquist again." Although her expression never changed, this time around, her voice sounded far less gruff.

Jackson looked over in the younger woman's direction to make sure he wasn't stepping on anyone's toes before he answered Miss Joan's question.

"Her brother Ryan's going to be staying at the ranch for a while."

Miss Joan's hazel eyes softened as they regarded the new woman at the counter for a moment. "Oh, I see. Well, it's a damn fine place to stay," the diner owner said to no one in particular and everyone in general. "Some pretty worthwhile people have put in their time at The Healing Ranch."

As she spoke, Miss Joan placed an empty cup and saucer on the counter, then proceeded to fill the cup with coffee that looked blacker than a raven's wing.

With the cup three-quarters full—leaving room for cream if any was desired—she moved it in front of the young woman Jackson had brought in.

Debi looked down at the cup. She was husbanding every dime she had. She couldn't afford to just throw money around, even for something as relatively inexpensive as a cup of coffee. Until she was assured of securing that job at the clinic that Jackson had told her about, every penny was precious and counted.

"I'm sorry, there's been a mistake. I didn't ask for any coffee," Debi told her politely, moving the cup and saucer back.

Miss Joan offered her a steely glimmer of a smile as she gently pushed the cup and saucer back in front of her. "First cup is always on the house," Miss Joan told her. "House rules," she added in case more of a protest was coming.

Debi found the woman's smile a little unnerving. A frown looked to be more at home on the woman's lean face, she couldn't help thinking.

She gave it half a minute. The smile, such as it was, remained. Maybe the woman's offer was on the level, Debi decided.

"Thank you," Debi murmured, bringing the coffee closer to her. It smelled delicious.

"You can sit, you know," Miss Joan told her, gesturing

at the empty stools that were directly behind her. "There's no extra charge for that."

As if on cue—and to show her how it was done—Jackson slid onto the stool that was next to the one behind her.

At this point, standing there was beginning to make her feel awkward, so Debi slid onto the stool that was right behind her.

Miss Joan moved both the creamer and the shaker of sugar over to her. The brief flash of a smile seemed to say that the diner owner knew she was a cream-and-sugar person.

"So, where are you from?" Miss Joan asked without the slightest bit of hesitation, or even the hint of a preamble.

Debi took a long sip of coffee first before answering quietly, "Indianapolis."

Miss Joan's expression gave nothing away. "Nice place to be from," she agreed. "Dropping the boy off and going back?" she questioned casually.

Debi's immediate reaction was to say that that was no one's business except for the man who had brought her here, and that was only because he would need to know how to get in touch with her. But the survival instincts that had gotten her this far warned Debi that her words might give offense to the woman. She had the very strong feeling that Miss Joan was someone she would rather have on her side than not.

"No, I'm going to stay in Forever until Mr. White Eagle thinks Ryan can be taken home." God, but that made Ryan sound like he was a cake or something. When a cake was baked and cooled, then it could be transported.

Miss Joan looked over toward Jackson, then back to the young woman he'd brought with him. "Mr. White Eagle, eh?" Miss Joan chuckled to herself, clearly amused. And then she became more businesslike again. "You know, I could use a little help behind the counter," she said, approaching the offer she was about to make slowly and tendering it to Jackson as if he was the intermediary in this scenario. "Nothing major, just a few hours a day. Maybe some help with the inventory," she added, her eyes meeting Jackson's.

"Debi's a surgical nurse," Jackson told the older woman. "I'm going to bring her to the clinic since they could always use some help." His mouth curved into an easy, friendly smile, one she hadn't witnessed yet, Debi caught herself thinking. "But I thought she should meet the queen bee first."

Miss Joan leveled a long, scrutinizing gaze at the young man she had known since before he took his first step, thanks to Sam.

She pretended to be displeased with the label he had just given her. "Don't get sassy with me, boy. If I were 'the queen bee,' you can bet your bottom that I would have stung you a long time ago."

Debi looked from the woman to Jackson, wondering if this was an argument because of her, or if Miss Joan was just bandying words about. The woman didn't appear to be particularly annoyed. Then again, Debi really didn't know her at all. Maybe this *was* the older woman's annoyed expression.

Unable to decide, Debi took refuge in the cup of coffee that Miss Joan had placed before her. The coffee was light enough, but it still hadn't reached its maximum sweetness level. She added another teaspoon of sugar, then took another tentative sip. Satisfied with the results, Debi drank up in earnest.

Aware that the woman was watching her—and rather intently at that—she assumed that Miss Joan wanted to know what she thought of the coffee, so she offered her a smile and murmured, "Good."

The corners of Miss Joan's thin lips curved so slightly anyone with challenged eyesight would *not* have been able to detect the difference.

"I know," she replied as she went back to her other customers, leaving the duo alone.

For now.

"Did I pass inspection?" Debi asked in a whisper, holding the cup in front of her lips so that if Miss Joan looked over in her direction, the woman wouldn't see them moving. There was no doubt in Debi's mind that Miss Joan probably knew how to read lips.

Amusement glinted in Jackson's deep sky-blue eyes. "Yes."

He sounded convinced. However, she wasn't. Just what did he know that she didn't? Or was he just trying to placate her?

"How can you tell?" Debi asked.

Jackson smiled, his amusement very evident. For just a second, he felt like a guide, unveiling a national treasure. Had circumstances been different, he could have been talking to Debi about his aunt instead of just the very unique and unorthodox owner of the town's only restaurant.

"If you didn't," he told her knowingly, "you would have heard about it. Trust me." Having finished his own cup of coffee, he gave no indication that he was about to get up. Instead, he nodded at her cup. "When you're finished, I'll take you to the clinic."

Debi was eager to have her situation resolved and on an even keel—or as even a keel as her circumstances allowed. She drained the rest of her coffee with one long swig. Swallowing, she set the cup down in its saucer, and said, "Finished."

Jackson suppressed a laugh. He hadn't expected her to gulp down her coffee.

This woman might be interesting after all.

"Then I guess we're good to go," he responded.

Jackson finished the last of his own coffee and set the cup down. Looking about the diner, he saw Miss Joan and nodded at the woman as if to say goodbye.

The next second, he was leading the way to the door. He didn't expect to have Debi suddenly ease herself in front of him and go outside first.

Why was she in such a hurry? Was it merely because she was anxious about getting a job at the clinic—or was there another reason for her all but racing outside of the diner?

Debi squeezed past the cowboy and went through the exit first. When he joined her outside the silver structure, she turned around and blurted out, "Is she like that with everyone?"

Now he understood her hurry to leave the diner. For some, Miss Joan was an acquired taste. Even he would admit that the woman did take some getting used to.

When his stepmother had died, Miss Joan had stepped in, like family, and had taken care of details he would have never even thought to attend to. Without so many words, she was there to provide emotional support, as well, if either he or Garrett needed it. In Garrett's case,

Sylvia had been his mother, so making it through the first few days and then weeks had been difficult—and would have been even more so without Miss Joan.

"Absolutely," he was quick to assure her. "You always know where you stand with Miss Joan. She doesn't believe in playing games or fabricating stories. Miss Joan is the real deal," he told Debi. And then, as if reading her mind, he added, "She can come on pretty crusty at times."

Now *that* was an understatement if she'd ever heard one. "I'll say."

"But there's nobody I'd rather have in my corner," he said with conviction. "When she's with you, she's with you a hundred and ten percent. Not to mention that the woman has a heart of gold."

He could see that Debi needed convincing of that. Jackson thought of telling her about Sylvia, but that felt too personal. Fortunately, there was more than one story.

"One winter was particularly bad here. Crops had failed, a lot of people were out of work. And things were particularly bad on the reservation. Miss Joan made sure her food trucks made it there every week until things turned around. Wouldn't take a penny, either. Said they could pay her when they were back on their feet. Turned out she was losing money right and left. But, being Miss Joan, she didn't say a word about it. When someone found out and asked how she could get by, she said that wasn't anyone's business but her own." He smiled to himself as he started up his truck again. It wasn't far from the diner to the clinic, but, being tired, he figured Debi would prefer not to walk. "A lot of folks around here think of her as the town's guardian angel. Nobody says anything like that to her face, of course, because they know she'll prob ably let loose with a string of words that would more than fill up ten swear jars," he told Debi. "Still, I think she'd be secretly tickled to hear that we think of her that way.

"Looks like they've got another full day," Jackson said in the next breath as he drew near the medical clinic. There were all manner of vehicles parked in front of the single-story building as well as close by. "You are really going to make their day," he predicted as he looked for a place to park.

I hope so, Debi thought, mentally crossing her fingers.

Chapter Seven

Holly Rodriguez pushed a wayward, stubborn strand of dark blond hair out of her blue eyes. It just annoyingly refused to stay put and she had no time to fuss with it. The day felt as if it was spinning out of control and she barely had time to breathe, much less fuss with her hair.

As happened on a tediously regular basis, she'd wound up pulling double duty at the clinic. That meant that she had to periodically return to the front desk and act as what had once been referred to, generations ago, as a "Girl Friday"—which meant that she had to do whatever it took to keep the office, or in this case, the clinic, running as smoothly as was humanly possible.

The rest of the time, she was in the back, working at her true calling and recently obtained vocation, that of being a nurse. Achieving the status meant that her fondest dream had come true. Or, more accurately, her fondest dream right after marrying Ray, the youngest of the Rodriguez clan and the man she had been in love with for what amounted to most of her life—ever since elementary school.

Holly loved being a nurse.

Loved it so much that not even the most menial of tasks associated with the vocation daunted her enthusi asm. On a few rare occasions, since Forever had no hospital and the closest one was located in Pine Ridge, some fifty miles away, patients who had to undergo emergency surgery were placed in the room that served as the clinic's recovery area. When that happened, Holly was the one who gladly remained overnight and watched over the patient until he or she was strong enough to be transported to Pine Ridge Memorial.

Holly had momentarily returned to the front desk less than three minutes ago. She was in the middle of organizing the last batch of patients who had signed in while she was in the back, assisting the two doctors. She had to admit, if only to herself, that trying to split herself equally between the doctors and working the desk was really beginning to wear her down.

Right about now, she was very close to wanting to sell her soul for some extra help.

The bell over the door chimed, indicating that yet another patient was coming in. Holly tried not to feel overwhelmed as she looked up to see who had come hoping to be squeezed in to see one of the doctors.

It felt as if most of Forever had already been here today.

Holly was surprised to see Jackson White Eagle enter. To her recollection, the man had never set foot in the clinic seeking medical help for himself. It was always for whomever he had in tow.

Today was no different, Holly thought when she saw that someone was with him.

Someone, Holly realized as she looked more closely, who she didn't recognize at all.

Between working at the clinic and waitressing at the diner, the job she'd held down while she was studying for her nursing degree, Holly felt fairly confident that she knew everyone who lived in and around Forever, at least by sight if not by actual name.

But the person with Jackson was a woman she had never seen before.

"You picked a really bad day to try to see one of the doctors," she told Jackson the moment he crossed to the front desk. "I think we're well on our way to breaking the record for number of patients treated here in a single day. If you're not feeling too bad, maybe you could come back tomorrow," Holly tactfully suggested. She was addressing her words to Jackson, but due to past experience, the polite suggestion was intended for the person she assumed was the real patient, the woman he had brought in with him.

"We're not sick," Jackson assured her. "As a matter of fact, I'm actually here to do you and the docs a favor."

A rather mysterious smile played on his lips as he spoke.

Somewhat confused, Holly cocked her head, waiting for more of an explanation.

"Who's in charge of hiring?" Jackson asked her.

He assumed that it was Dr. Davenport, since Davenport was the one who had reopened the clinic after it had been closed for over thirty years. But just in case Dan had handed off that job to the new doctor, he didn't want to start Debi off on the wrong foot by accidentally stepping on any toes—or egos.

But he hadn't.

"That would be Dr. Dan. Why do you ask?" Holly asked. The words were no sooner out of her mouth than the answer hit her. Afraid that she'd probably made a mistake, her eyes still seemed to light up as she went on to ask, "Did you bring the clinic a sec— An adminis-trative assistant?"

Her tongue had stumbled a little over the job title. At times it was hard remembering the correct terminology being used these days. Forever might be a very small town with its share of growing pains, but it wasn't ex-actly lost in the last century, either. People in the know did their best to remain current.

Jackson glanced at the woman with him before look-ing back at Holly. There was a spark of amusement in his eyes. "Not exactly."

"Oh." The single word was just brimming with dis-appointment.

Debi was quick to pick up on it—as well as to take in the fact that there was growing chaos on the front desk's surface.

"Do you need help out here?" Debi asked, ready to volunteer.

She knew what it felt like to be swamped. As far as she was concerned, what she'd just asked was basically a rhetorical question since she could see that the young woman behind the front desk was all but drowning in paperwork, files and patients.

"Oh, God, yes." The words slipped out of Holly's mouth before she could think to stop them. She could handle this, she knew she could. It would just take her half the night after the doors closed, that's all.

The young woman's response was all the urging Debi needed. "What do you need me to do?" she asked, com-ing around the desk.

Jackson watched the woman he'd brought to the clinic. It was his turn to be confused. "I thought you told me that you were a surgical nurse," Jackson said.

"I am, but I worked in the front office while I was studying for my nursing degree. You get a feel for how a hospital operates that way."

Holly's mouth dropped open.

"You're a nurse?" she cried, looking very much like a child whose every wish for Christmas had just been summarily granted. "Really?" Her voice trailed off in a thrilled squeak.

"Really," Debi happily confirmed, then added, "But I know my way around a desk and appointment ledgers. I don't mind working a desk, really."

Energized by this one piece of information and the promise that went with it, Holly sprang to her feet. "Wait right here," she instructed both of them.

Actually, it was more of a plea.

She began to dash to the back of the clinic when one of the patients in the waiting room lumbered to his feet. A big man with a gravelly voice, Ralph Walters wasn't shy about voicing his displeasure.

"Hey, I've been waiting to see the doctor for almost an hour," he complained, then jerked his thumb in Jackson's direction. "How come they're getting to see him before I do?"

"Because they're about to make life a whole lot better around here," Holly promised. Turning around to look at Jackson and the young woman he had brought with him, she said, "Don't go anywhere."

The next moment, she ducked into the second exam room.

Less than three minutes later, Holly was back out and at the desk. "Dr. Dan said not to go anywhere. He's finishing up with a patient and he'll be right out to see you."

Debi realized that with all this going on around her,

she hadn't introduced herself to the very pretty, harried young woman behind the desk. Leaning forward, she extended her hand to the nurse.

"Hi, I'm Debi Kincannon," she told her.

Holly grinned. "I'm Holly Rodriguez," she responded, gladly taking Debi's hand and shaking it.

"And I'm getting damn impatient," Ralph grumbled, glaring at the two women.

Holly suppressed a sigh. "Mr. Walters, please. The doctors are working as quickly as they can, but they don't want to be careless or overlook something just in order to save time," Holly told him, doing her best to reason with the man.

Jackson turned around and looked at Walters, who had a couple of inches and a great many pounds on him. Seeing what appeared to have all the earmarks of a confrontation, Debi held her breath as she waited to see just what was going to happen next.

"Nobody likes waiting, Mr. Walters," Jackson pointed out. "But complaining about it just makes it unpleasant for everyone."

Walters appeared as if he was about to say a few choice words in response, but then the older man looked up into Jackson's face. It was obvious that the rancher realized that Jackson was younger, stronger and far more capable of subduing him than the other way around.

Muttering under his breath rather than voicing his opinion out loud, Walters sank back down into his seat again.

Holly seemed both impressed at the interaction and relieved that it hadn't escalated. "Bless you," she mouthed to Jackson.

Jackson nodded in reply.

Just then, the door to the second exam room opened

and Alice Ledbetter, one of Miss Joan's waitresses, walked out. The woman was smiling. "My back and neck feel much better already," she was saying to the tall, striking man who walked out with her. "I don't know how to thank you, Doctor."

"That's what I'm here for," Dan replied genially. Sending off his patient, Dan quickly took in the duo standing by the front desk. "Jackson," he said heartily, shaking the man's hand, "Holly tells me that you've brought someone to make our lives here a little less hectic." Dan focused on the young woman standing beside Jackson. "I take it Jackson and Holly were talking about you."

Flattered and a little floored, Debi wasn't exactly sure just what to say or even where to begin. Did she thank the man for seeing her? Modestly brush aside the fact that any sort of compliments were implied? Or did she give him a litany of her accomplishments and focus on explaining why he should be hiring her?

In general, she had never been the type to oversell herself. Too much of a buildup left too much of an opportunity for a letdown. She could only go with the simple truth.

"I'm a surgical nurse and I'm going to be here in Forever for at least a month." She glanced toward Jackson. Maybe she was being too optimistic about Ryan's progress. "Maybe longer. I was wondering if you—"

"You're hired," Dan told her.

Debi stared at him, stunned. She was good and she deserved to be hired, but there was no way the man could know that, not without verification.

"Don't you want references, to see my work records, my—"

Dan stopped her right there.

"I'm sure they're all in order. If they're not, that'll come to light quickly enough," Dan told her. Putting out his hand to her, he said, "I'm Dan Davenport and I'm very happy for any help you can give us, as, I'm sure, is Holly. We'll discuss terms later after the clinic closes for the night. When can you start?" he asked, not bothering to hide the fact that he was eager for her to join the team.

"I was thinking tomorrow, but I can stay and help Holly if she needs me to." Debi was exhausted and the thought of getting a room at the hotel and just sleeping through until tomorrow morning had a great deal of appeal, but becoming part of the team, even a temporary member, was important. She didn't want to begin by shirking off responsibility.

"And risk having you quit before you ever get started?" Dan asked with a laugh. "No, tomorrow will be fine," he told her. About to go into exam room one where yet another patient was waiting for him, Dan paused for a moment longer as a question occurred to him. "Do you have a place to stay? Because if you don't, my wife and I have a spare bedroom—"

"I'm taking her to the hotel," Jackson told him, cutting the doctor's offer short.

Dan nodded. "Good—but if you decide you don't like it there, the offer's still on the table," he told his new nurse before finally leaving the reception area.

Holly was about to bring another patient into the room that Alice Ledbetter had just vacated. But first she paused for a moment by the woman she looked upon as a candidate to become her new best friend.

"Ray and I have plenty of room on the ranch if you decide you want something a little quieter than a room at the hotel," she offered. "No charge," she promised. "Just let me know."

Debi nodded, somewhat caught off guard by the displays of generosity aimed in her direction. It overwhelmed her.

"You look a little confused," Jackson observed as they walked out of the clinic again. Despite the Stetson he wore, Jackson found he had to shade his eyes as he looked in her direction. "Something wrong?"

She wouldn't have put it quite that way. "Not wrong, exactly…"

Inclining his head, he asked her patiently, "But what, 'exactly'?"

She wasn't used to being on the receiving end of this sort of selfless generosity. It didn't exactly make her feel uncomfortable, but it did make her feel a little…strange, for lack of a better word to describe her reaction.

Debi did her best to explain how she felt about being offered all of this to Jackson.

"Where I come from, people go out of their way *not* to take you in if they don't have to, especially if they don't really know you. Being offered a place to stay not once but twice in the space of a few minutes, well, it just seems…"

Her voice trailed off as she lifted her shoulders in a vague shrug.

"Unusually generous?" he supplied when she stopped talking.

Debi nodded. That was as good a way to phrase it as any, she supposed. "That wasn't exactly what I was going to say, but I guess that's a good way to describe it."

"I guess people are a little more cautious about open

ing up their homes to other people in Indianapolis," Jackson guessed.

"Yes."

Was he looking down at Indianapolis? She could feel herself automatically getting defensive. When had defensiveness become a way of life? she wondered. It hadn't always been that way.

"People tend to march to a different beat in a big city. In a town, especially a town as small as Forever is, people look out for one another." It was the same way on a reservation, Jackson thought. Because they had more than their share of missing parents and incomplete family units, the inhabitants that were there became one large extended family. "It's the usual course of events. They want to help, they get involved. Anonymity and minding 'your own business' just isn't a factor in a small town like Forever."

"Maybe not, but it does take some getting used to," Debi confessed.

He thought about it for a moment. "I suppose that it does. If you're raised to be suspicious and to examine everything, then taking things at face value takes some effort."

Something in his voice caught her attention. "You sound like you've been through something like that yourself."

She regarded him in a whole new light. Initially, she'd thought that Jackson was born somewhere close by if not directly in Forever. But for him to know why she might have misgivings about the offers that had been made, he had to have experienced something along the same lines as she had at some point.

"I might," Jackson acknowledged, then closed the topic in the next moment. "Here's the hotel," he announced needlessly.

The hotel had been finished less than a year ago and it was still a surprise to see it standing there whenever he came into town. Getting used to having the building as part of the town's backdrop was going to take some doing, Jackson surmised.

"You know, if you're worried about money," he began abruptly as he pulled up in front of the hotel, "you're welcome to stay on the ranch."

"Your ranch?" she asked, half convinced that he had to be referring to another one.

"Yes," he answered. Why would she think that he would offer up someone else's home?

"Where?" To the best of her knowledge, any extra people on the ranch slept in one communal place. "In the bunkhouse?"

Now *that* would have definitely been asking for trouble, Jackson thought.

"No, we can't have you staying there with the guys. If nothing else, that sends the wrong message to them and having you there would definitely distract them from any lesson they've been sent here to learn. No, I was talking about the ranch house," he told her. "We do have a couple of spare bedrooms in the ranch house. Nothing fancy, just a bed, a small bureau and one nightstand." He came full circle back to the reason for the offer. "But if you're pressed for money—"

Debi looked at him, surprised and somewhat uncomfortable.

"Who said I was pressed for money?" she asked.

"No one," he replied simply.

He wasn't making his offer based on words he had actually heard. What had prompted him to make the offer was a feeling he'd gotten from the way she talked more than from what she actually said. She'd said she was taking a leave of absence from her job, but she had seemed eager to go to work at the clinic. If money was of no consequence, she would have been content just to stay at the hotel and observe Ryan at a distance.

Money, however, *was* of consequence.

"But no one likes to spend money if they don't have to…" he said vaguely.

She had a difference of opinion on that, an opinion that was probably the direct opposite of the one that Jackson had, she thought. She knew of several people who loved spending money and they did it as if it was going out of style.

In addition, one of those people—John—was actually spending money he didn't have. That had come to light thanks to the divorce proceedings. Spending money recklessly was definitely something she would absolutely *never* do. However, she wasn't about to be the object of pity, either. If she actually did have that job at the clinic, then the charge for the hotel room wouldn't be a problem. She wasn't looking to save money while here, she was attempting to pay her bills while she stayed close enough to be within shouting range for Ryan if it turned out that he needed her.

"If I'm going to be working at the clinic, it's easier for me to be staying in town, as well, which in this case means having a room in the hotel. But thanks for the offer," she told him with feeling.

Jackson shrugged. "Don't mention it. Anytime I can

make you an offer you don't want to take me up on, just let me know."

He noticed that her eyes crinkled as she laughed softly to herself. "I'll be sure to do that," she told him.

Chapter Eight

Jackson walked into the bunkhouse, the heels of his boots echoing within the all but empty room.

He'd been expecting this.

Expecting the challenge from the newcomer. The contest of wills that pitted the newcomer against the authority figure—in this case, him. New "ranch hands" always envisioned the clash they felt was coming, the one they always built up in their minds because it was all they had to cling to. It was crucial to their so-called hot-shot reputations which made them the king of the hill.

Or so they believed.

Debi Kincannon's brother, Ryan, struck him as being no different from all the other boys he had taken on at the ranch since he'd started his program. Boys who arrived with attitude to spare stuffed into their suitcases because their self-esteem was nonexistent.

Oh, there were nuanced differences to be detected, because every boy was different in some way. But when it came to the overall big picture, all the boys were basically alike. They felt neglected, ignored, belittled, and they were all bent on doing something to be noticed, something that would gain them a measure of respect, even in a cursory, shallow way.

It was better than nothing.

And every troubled teen who, one way or another, found his way to The Healing Ranch would challenge his authority, sometimes immediately, sometimes a little later, but most of the time sooner than later.

Ryan, apparently, wanted to start that way right off the bat.

As he crossed the bunkhouse floor, making his way to the two rows of beds facing one another, Jackson spotted Debi's brother immediately. Ryan was sitting on his bunk with his back against the wall.

His arms were crossed before his thin, shallow chest, a bantam rooster biding his time and waiting for the fight to start.

Jackson could feel the teen's dark brown eyes on him, watching his every move.

Waiting.

So it was up to him to break the silence, Jackson thought. He obliged. "Garrett said you refused to leave your bunk."

Ryan's lower lip curled in a smirk. "Yeah, he's smart that way," the teen quipped. Something flickered in his eyes. Fear? "Don't think you can get me up, 'cause I got ways to hurt you."

"I'm not about to drag you out of bed," Jackson told the teenager. "Although I could if I wanted to," he informed him in a steely, unemotional voice. Letting him know the way things could be. "But if that's what you want to do, lie in bed all day, be my guest."

"Why are you being so nice?" Ryan asked suspiciously, pressing his back even harder against the wall, as if bracing himself for a sudden move.

Jackson shrugged indifferently. "I'm not being nice. Just the opposite."

More suspicion, if possible, entered Ryan's eyes. "How do you figure that?"

"Well, if I was being nice," Jackson said, coming to a stop directly in front of Ryan's bunk bed, "you'd be able to eat lunch and dinner."

Ryan scowled at him. "Why can't I eat?" he asked.

Jackson's tone indicated that the answer was self-explanatory. "Because you've elected to lie in bed. You don't work, you don't eat. It's as simple as that. There are no free rides here, Ryan. You have to earn everything, just like in the world that exists outside these walls."

Ryan raised his chin. "My sister's not going to let you starve me," he cried.

"She has no say in it," Jackson said in a soft voice that was all the more terrifying for its lack of volume. "Your sister signed over all rights over you to me. While you're here, I am your sole guardian." He was stretching things, but he knew that Ryan had no way of knowing that. "I decide what you do, what you wear, if you eat. I decide *everything*."

Clearly, Ryan's fear was escalating. "I don't believe you," he cried. "Deb wouldn't do that."

Jackson didn't bother trying to convince him, didn't waste so much as a single breath arguing, cajoling or convincing. Instead, he took a folded, legal-looking document out of his back pocket and held it out for Ryan to see.

"That's your sister's signature, isn't it?" he asked calmly.

Ryan's breath shortened and caught in his throat, and he looked to be on the verge of a screaming fit. Jumping up out of the bunk, Ryan looked around for something to throw, to break.

Grabbing the first thing he saw, a lamp, he was all set to throw it when Jackson informed him, "You break it, you pay for it. And if you have no coinage because you refuse to work here, you'll wind up spending a few days in jail as a guest of the county."

"You can't do that." Ryan's voice cracked as he spat out the retort.

"Oh, but I can," Jackson countered.

On his feet, the teen looked like a caged wild animal, scanning the room as he tried to figure out his next-best move.

There wasn't one.

Undoubtedly, he hated conceding, but it appeared that he had no choice. "So if I work, I eat?"

"That's the deal," Jackson agreed.

"And this 'work' you're talking about," he said, approaching the subject warily, "just what is it that I do?"

"It varies. Whatever is on your schedule to do that day," Jackson told him.

Muttering something unintelligible, Ryan stomped toward the door, anger smoldering in his eyes.

"Oh, and if you don't put in a full day," Jackson added as Ryan passed him, "you get docked for each half hour you miss."

Ryan swung around to glare at his jailer. "You've got this damn thing rigged, don't you?"

"You owe another dollar to the swear jar," he said mildly. "And as for what you just said, it works both ways," Jackson answered, his tone as mild as when he had begun talking.

While The Healing Ranch was still in its early days,

he'd discovered that the boys he had undertaken to turn around behaviorally had a great deal in common with wild animals.

And as with wild animals, if he spoke in a non-threatening, even an almost monotone, sort of way, there would be far less miscommunication between them.

"But all we can hope for is the present and the future. There is no changing the past," Jackson murmured under his breath to himself as he walked out of the bunkhouse behind Ryan.

Out in the open, the teen turned around and looked accusingly at him. "So where am I supposed to be today?" he asked in a nasty tone.

That was an easy enough question to answer. He had checked all the teens' schedules first thing that morning, before he had even gotten dressed or sat down to his own breakfast. "You have stable duty."

"Wow, what a surprise," Ryan sneered. He looked around the area and saw some of the other teenagers he had bunked with last night. They were in the corral, each of them working with the horse that had been assigned to them. For a moment, it appeared as if interest had sparked in his eyes before he reassumed his bored, sullen stance. "Hey—" he swung around to look at Jackson "—when do I get my own horse?"

"When you've earned it," Jackson replied matter-of-factly.

Lengthening his stride, he passed Ryan and made his way over to the corral to see how the teens there were doing.

"And how do I accomplish that great deed, oh Fearless Leader?" The sarcasm fairly dripped from Ryan's lips as he asked the question.

"I'll let you know when it happens, Ryan," Jackson told him.

Frustrated and obviously feeling helpless, Ryan raised his voice and shouted after Jackson, his tone threatening, "I'm going to tell my sister that you're just yanking me around!"

Without breaking stride, Jackson turned for a split second and calmly called back, "Won't make any difference, remember?"

The next minute, Jackson behaved like a man who was completely out of earshot, even though in reality he could actually hear everything that the teen was shouting at him.

He'd made himself immune to words the likes of which Ryan was hurling at him a long time ago.

"How long?" Garrett asked him, joining his brother as Jackson reached the perimeter of the corral.

Jackson knew exactly what Garrett was asking. He barely paused to think. His response at this point, after all the boys he and Garrett had worked with and managed to turn around, was close to a science and his assessments were all but automatic.

"A week, week and a half if he's particularly stubborn."

"A week and a half before he drops that abrasive attitude." Shaking his head, Garrett sighed. "Tell me again why we keep beating our heads against the wall, trying to make model citizens out of a bunch of thugs, future con men and thieves?"

"We're banging our heads against the wall because we want to keep them from becoming those future con men and thieves. We make a difference, Garrett," Jackson stressed. "And we're banging our heads against the wall because when *we* were these rotten know-it-alls, Sam was there for us. And *because* he was—and because he turned us around—now it's our turn to be there for all those others who don't have an Uncle Sam—no word-play intended," he added when he realized what that had to sound like.

Leaning against the corral railings, Jackson momentarily allowed his thoughts to drift back to his much earlier days. He'd lived on the reservation then and all he had wanted back in those days was to fit in, to be accepted.

"Besides," he continued as if this, at bottom, had been the answer to Garrett's question all along. "Weren't you the one who said he liked that good feeling inside when he realized he'd turned another kid around and kept him away from a life of crime?"

"Maybe." Garrett shrugged his shoulders carelessly. "I guess I must have had one too many beers when I said that."

Jackson played along. "Doesn't matter if you did or not. The point is that you said it and since you did, it can't be unsaid. You're committed to this way of life, same as I am." He was well aware of the fact that he couldn't have done nearly as much as he had if Garrett hadn't been there right next to him, sharing the load. "Repeat after me," he coaxed Garrett. "It's nice to make a difference."

"'It's nice to make a difference,'" Garrett parroted. "It would be even *nicer* to be well compensated for it," he added with a bit more feeling than he had intended to begin with.

"We are," Jackson told him in all sincerity. "It just doesn't happen to be in coinage."

"Ever try to buy dinner with non-coinage?" Garrett

asked him. He frowned slightly as he went on to say, "Doesn't work very well."

Jackson stopped watching the teens in the corral and looked at Garrett more closely for the first time during their conversation. "You're serious, aren't you?" He eyed Garrett with concern. "Are you burned-out?"

Garrett shrugged.

"Let's just say, it's more like tapped out."

"We're not in this for the money," Jackson reminded him.

Garrett laughed shortly. "Hell, don't I know *that*," he said.

Jackson had always believed in tackling a problem head-on, before it became a major disaster. If nothing else, he wanted to be prepared for whatever this problem might happen to kick up.

"You thinking of leaving the ranch?" Jackson asked, hoping he'd managed to successfully hide his deep concern.

"I'm *always* thinking of leaving," Garrett confided to his brother.

He supposed that wasn't exactly a secret, Jackson thought. Hell, there were times when he was all set to pack his own bags and go himself. But the good accomplished on the ranch far outweighed the bad he had to endure. It always did, which was why he was hopeful about continuing their work.

"Well, before you act on it, Garrett, come talk to me," Jackson requested.

"Right, because you're really talkative and everything." Garrett laughed, shaking his head.

"Good point," Jackson responded. He certainly couldn't dispute his brother's image of him. He'd always believed in an economy of words. The world was already far too littered with words uttered by people who just liked to hear the sound of their own voices.

"I said come talk to me, I didn't say I'd talk back. Sometimes you just need someone to listen and use as a sounding board, nothing more."

"And you can be as wooden as the best of them," Garrett guessed, laughing heartily.

"Now you've got it," Jackson told his brother with an affectionate grin. But, being Jackson, the grin vanished even before it fully registered on his lips.

Just another day at the ranch, Jackson thought, leaving Garrett and moving on to interact with the teens in the corral.

DEBI REALIZED THAT she had never totally appreciated what "putting in a full day's work" actually meant until today.

She had definitely put in a very full day at the clinic.

It was a little like being thrown headfirst into the deep end of the pool—except in that case, even if she were a nonswimmer, she'd still had reasonable expectations of survival.

Here at the clinic, it was a somewhat different story. Midway through her first day, she wasn't all that sure about her odds of surviving until sunset.

The pace at County General, the hospital where she worked back in Indianapolis, had always been rather hectic with very little downtime, but there *was* downtime on occasion. She had a very strong suspicion that "downtime" here at the clinic would have to involve some sort of an injury that would normally keep her off her feet—and even then the doctor in charge, Dan Davenport, would probably urge her to keep on going, injury or not, cast or no cast.

It wasn't that Davenport was a slave driver—he seemed like a very nice person. As was everyone else who worked at the clinic.

The second she walked into the place, believing herself to be twenty minutes early, she saw a line of people beginning at the door and spilling out onto the street. It just became worse once the clinic doors opened. The people just kept on coming.

Eventually she decided that there had to be an endless supply of sick people within the town because for every one examined, two more came to take his or her place.

Try as they might, the doctors still couldn't get to all of the patients during normal working hours. But rather than send them away the way she assumed that they would, the doctors had her lock the front doors as an indication that they weren't accepting any more walk-ins. Then the patients who were still in the clinic, despite the fact that the hours of operation were over, were seen, each and every one of them. Neither doctor gave any indication that they would leave before the last of the patients were examined and diagnosed.

Dedication like that could be truly wonderful when there was no one waiting at home for you to come through the door. In that case, it allowed a person to give as much of themselves as they wanted to.

However, she quickly learned that was not the case for either of the doctors, or Holly for that matter. All three had spouses and children at home waiting for them.

She was the only one who had no one.

Coming "home" to the hotel room held no allure for her. Oh, the room itself was quite lovely. And it was also small, the perfect size for one occupant, not so much for two. She supposed she was given this one intentionally so as not to emphasize the emptiness of both the room and the life of the person who temporarily occupied it.

She had gotten so used to being someone's wife, to thinking in terms of two rather than just one, she found herself missing being married. Not missing John, just missing the concept of being married.

Which was why, she silently reminded herself, she needed to work, to keep occupied. To that end, Jackson White Eagle had done her a huge favor by bringing her to the clinic.

But she had reached her saturation point. Although she'd wanted to be a nurse for as far back as she could remember, right now she knew if she saw one more patient, applied one more cuff to measure blood pressure or called in one more prescription to be filled, she was going to run into the streets, screaming out words that the children in the area did not need to hear.

Before she had become a surgical nurse, she had worked in the ER. She had been convinced that working in the ER had been rough. But compared to the day she had put in here at the clinic, a day in the ER seemed to her like a day spent at an amusement park.

Every bone in her body was beyond tired.

The doctors had finally removed their white lab coats and resumed their civilian lives. Holly had stayed to lock up and, as the "new kid on the block," Debi felt that she needed to remain, as well.

They were the last two to leave the building.

"You did great for your first day," Holly told her with weary cheerfulness.

Debi thought there was no harm in pushing the envelope just a little further. "How would you have said I did if this hadn't been my first day?"

Holly looked at her as if she thought that was a very odd question.

"Good, still good," she answered with as much enthusiasm as she could muster. "Glad to have you on our team for as long as you're going to be here in our area," Holly tacked on.

Everyone at the clinic—the doctors, Holly and the patients, as well—had made her feel welcome.

Exhausted, but welcome, she thought with a weary smile on her lips.

She and Holly parted at the door. Their cars were parked facing opposite directions. Holly was headed out of Forever to the ranch where she lived with her husband, her niece and her mother, while Debi had a far shorter drive to the hotel.

When she drew closer to her dusty car, Debi saw that there was someone leaning against the hood, his arms folded before his chest.

The arms gave him away. Standing like that, he looked more like a fierce warrior than a teacher schooled in brokering a peaceful coexistence between the teens sent to his ranch.

"Jackson?" she asked, almost hoping that it wasn't. If he was here, waiting for her, that meant that something had gone wrong with Ryan. That was the way she thought these days—because she was usually right. "Did something happen to Ryan?"

Jackson straightened up. "Other than learning that he can't have his way, no, nothing happened."

She didn't understand. "Then why are you here?"

"I just came by to see how you survived your first day at the clinic," he explained amicably.

It was a perfectly plausible excuse for his being here. Why she suddenly felt butterflies fluttering in her stomach was something she didn't feel she could explore. Not safely, anyway.

Chapter Nine

The next moment she looked at Jackson warily, not certain if she really believed his initial disclaimer. Maybe he was just trying to break something to her gently because he thought she might be the type to come unglued if something bad happened, like Ryan taking off without warning.

"And you're sure that this doesn't have anything to do with Ryan?" she asked, watching him carefully.

"Well, you wouldn't be here in Forever if it wasn't because of Ryan, so in a way it *is* related to Ryan—but only in the loosest sense of the meaning." By now, he was pretty aware of the way a parent's mind worked and the kinds of concerns that sprang to their minds. "If you're asking me if he's run off or done something to get thrown off the program—"

"Has he?" she asked almost breathlessly.

God, but her eyes were green. They had opened so wide, he felt as if he could just fall into them and then try to wade his way back to shore.

The next moment, Jackson upbraided himself sternly. *Get a grip*, he chided himself silently. *Remember your place. She's the sister of one of your charges. That means keep your distance.*

Doing anything else, he knew, would just be asking for trouble.

"No," he answered Debi quietly. "I left your brother on the ranch with the other ranch hands."

"Who's watching him?" she asked.

She knew Ryan. He could take off at a moment's notice—although where he could go in an area that had nothing to offer for miles in any direction was beyond her. But if Ryan felt wronged and was angry enough, he wouldn't think things through that far.

He'd just go.

"The other ranch hands," Jackson repeated. He sounded as calm as she was panicked. "They watch out for one another."

"Are you crazy?" Debi demanded, stunned. "They're all teenage boys. Having them watch each other, that's like throwing a match into a factory that makes fireworks."

"I'd give them a little more credit than that," he told her. For the most part, the teens had earned his complete trust. "Relax. I also left Garrett with them."

"Oh." She breathed a huge sigh of relief. "That's better."

He watched her, debating whether or not to point out the obvious. He decided that it was worth it—for her own good. "If the ranch hands were as bent on running away as you think, Garrett wouldn't be able to stop them. The odds would be against him."

From what little she'd seen, Garrett seemed as if he could handle himself. But Jackson, in her estimation, looked to be even better equipped to cope with the boys. "But not against you," she guessed.

"Fortunately for us, nobody's ever tested that theory.

And right now, after the day they've all put in, I'd say they're all too tired to lift their feet, much less make a break for it."

She could certainly relate to that, Debi thought.

"In any case, I didn't come to talk about the ranch," he reminded her. "How did it go?"

Debi turned so that she could see the darkened clinic from where she stood. It looked deceptively quiet—now. "It went," she remarked. "Someone said that the clinic hasn't been here all that long."

"It hasn't," Jackson confirmed.

"Where did the doctors practice, then?"

"They didn't," he told her. He liked the way surprise added a touch of innocence to Debi's face. "Dr. Dan came out here a few years ago. Something about taking his brother's place because his brother was supposed to come here but died in a car accident the night before he was supposed to leave." He paused for a moment to think. "Lady Doc's only been here less than a year."

"Lady Doc?"

"That's what her husband, Brett, called her the first time he met her. It kinda stuck," Jackson explained. "Holly's the only native from around here," he said, referring to the lone nurse.

Debi was still having trouble processing what he'd told her to begin with. "If neither of the doctors have been here all that long, what did the people do before that?"

"Well, they either drove the fifty miles to Pine Ridge, or they toughed it out. You hungry?"

The man changed topics fast enough to give her whiplash. She didn't answer his question one way or the other. Instead, she gave him a rather neutral reply. "I thought I'd just grab something at the hotel."

In some ways, the hotel was still evolving. The actual structure had been completed months ago. However, some of the extras that Connie Carmichael-Murphy had envisioned had yet to become a reality.

"Unless you were planning to chew on a pillow," Jackson said, "you're out of luck."

Debi stared at him quizzically. "Why's that?"

"Well, the hotel's a work in progress and they haven't gotten around to building a restaurant inside. Everyone kind of feels that would be an insult to Miss Joan."

"Why's that?"

"Right now, the diner's the only place anyone can get a meal."

"Are you sure? I thought I saw this other place." She thought for a moment, remembering a bright neon light forming a name. "Murphy's, I think the sign said." She'd caught a fleeting glimpse of the place. It looked more like a tavern than a restaurant, but to the best of her knowledge, taverns served food.

"Murphy's is the local saloon," Jackson told her. "The Murphy boys have got a standing agreement with Miss Joan. She doesn't serve beer or any other kind of liquor in her place of business and they don't serve food—other than the standard peanuts at the bar."

"And the hotel really doesn't serve anything?" she asked incredulously. She hadn't bothered to check it out last night when she'd registered, and as for this morning, with her stomach all tied up in knots, the thought of breakfast had just made her want to throw up.

After having put in a very long day, Debi was no longer too nervous to eat, but now her choices were rather limited.

She played devil's advocate. "And if I don't want to eat

at the diner?" The diner was perfectly acceptable, but the idea that she didn't have a choice didn't sit well with her.

Jackson mulled over her question. "You could either drive the fifty miles into Pine Ridge," he told her, "or go to the local general store and get yourself something to put in between two pieces of bread." He gave her his advice on the matter, for whatever it was worth. "The diner's got a better selection and at least the food'll be hot."

The thought of something warm hitting her stomach did have its appeal. She supposed that it wouldn't hurt to go to the diner again. There was just one thing she was still unclear about.

"Are you offering to come with me?" she asked.

The shrug was completely noncommittal. "Thought you might want to have someone to talk to until you got to know some of the regulars."

After the day she had just put in, silence was more welcome than conversation, but she didn't want to seem rude. Jackson was obviously putting himself out for her— besides, if she was standoffish and rude to him, the man might decide to take it out on Ryan.

For a second, she thought about asking him if there were any consequences to turning his offer down, but then decided that doing so just might put the thought into Jackson's head if it hadn't occurred to him before.

So she forced a smile to her lips and murmured, "That's very thoughtful of you."

And, if she was being strictly honest with herself, sitting at a table across from Jackson White Eagle couldn't exactly be considered a hardship. The man was exceptionally easy on the eyes.

His facial features were all angles and planes with strong cheekbones. And he was fit, she couldn't help not ing. His arms, even through his work shirt, looked as if they were as hard as rocks.

It was easy to see that the man didn't just sit back and let the others do the heavy labor. He worked the ranch just as hard as, if not harder than the boys who were in his care.

"My truck's right over there," he told her, pointing it out for her benefit. "Don't worry, I'll bring you back to your car after dinner."

"I wasn't worried," she protested, secretly wondering how he could possibly know that she had been.

"Sorry, my mistake," he replied, letting her have her way.

It took less than five minutes to get to Miss Joan's diner. The entire area around the silver structure was filled with cars. Jackson parked in the first spot he could find.

Debi took in the scene. It looked as if half the cars in Forever were parked near the diner. Business was obviously booming.

"I guess when you've got a monopoly, people don't have much of a choice where they go to eat," she commented.

"There's that," Jackson allowed, although he was fairly convinced that if the cooking was bad, all but the people most inept in the kitchen would choose to remain home. "And Angel's cooking."

"Angel?" she asked, curious.

"Angel Rodriguez," he told her. "That's one of Miss Joan's two cooks." He was fairly convinced the woman could make dirt appetizing. He spared Debi a quick half smile. "She's from out of town, too. Like you."

"So people actually come here and stay?" Debi asked in surprise.

Not that she exactly had a wild social life back in Indianapolis, but she was fairly certain that the people in Forever rolled up the streets after ten o'clock.

The entire town struck her as the last word in boring.

Jackson watched her as if he was making a judgment based on what she'd just said. "Hard to believe, but true."

After exiting the truck, Jackson moved around to her door and opened it before she had a chance to get out on her own.

Debi glanced down at the hand he was extending to her. Taking it, she curled her fingers around it and got out. The hint of a tingling sensation that undulated through her felt oddly arousing and comforting at the same time.

Just her mind playing tricks on her.

"Your mother taught you well," she commented. When his eyes narrowed, she explained, "Your manners. Your mother did a good job teaching you manners."

It took effort not to sound bitter. Every so often, the emotion would raise its head unexpectedly, taking a chunk out of him when he least expected it.

"My mother didn't teach me anything at all," he corrected.

Her head jerked up just a beat before she realized her mistake.

"Oh, I'm sorry. I didn't mean to dig up any painful memories." Her shoulders rose and fell in a careless, helpless motion. "I have a habit of saying the wrong thing at the wrong time," she apologized, shifting uncomfortably.

"Who told you that?" he asked sharply.

Maybe she had picked the right man for the job of turning Ryan around. He certainly could intuit things.

"My ex," she told him after a beat. "He said I was a verbal klutz." She could almost hear John's voice in her head, saying something disapproving. Looking back, she wondered why she hadn't caught on to John's subtle self-esteem bashing sooner—before he had done such a number on her.

"I can see why he's your ex," Jackson commented. "He didn't exactly have very much going for him in the flattery department, did he?"

It wasn't loyalty but a need to not be pitied that had her being defensive. "John liked to call them as he saw them."

"As he saw them, huh?" Jackson questioned skeptically. "He was obviously myopic so I wouldn't give a lot of credence to what he said if I were you."

Debi was going to counter what he had just said to her but she was headed off at the pass and never got the chance.

"Well, look who's decided to give us another try," Miss Joan said heartily by way of a greeting as she passed the duo. Personally making the rounds to refill her customers' coffee mugs, Miss Joan was carrying a pot that was filled to the brim. "Grab a dinner menu," she instructed Jackson. "I'll be right with you. Two seats right over there." Miss Joan pointed to a cozy table for two over in the corner. "Grab them while you can. This time of the evening they're going fast."

With that, Miss Joan went to complete her rounds and fill every cup that required filling.

"Are you getting used to her yet?" Jackson asked her as they sat down at the table that Miss Joan had pointed out.

Debi had her doubts that that was possible.

"Does *anyone* get used to her? Ever?" Debi asked, trying as discreetly as possible to keep observing the redhead while planting herself on the seat that Miss Joan had singled out for them.

"Oh, sure," Jackson answered. "It'll happen without you even realizing it. One morning," he predicted, "you'll wake up and it'll seem as if Miss Joan has always been part of your life."

"I sincerely doubt I'll live that long," she replied.

She could protest all she wanted, Jackson thought. He knew better because he'd seen it happen time and again. Miss Joan had a way about her—and a heart of gold. The latter was not on display and only became evident after a sufficient amount of time had gone by and her gruff exterior had faded.

"You'll see," Jackson said more to himself than to her.

"Besides, you're forgetting that I'm only here as long as Ryan's on your ranch. Once you've straightened him out, my brother and I'll be going back to our old way of life."

Why was she so eager to get back to the scene of everything that had gone wrong for her? Jackson wondered. "And your old stress triggers."

"You're getting ready to tell me that Ryan's 'magical cure' only sticks if he stays here?" she guessed. "That once he leaves, he'll go back to his old habits?"

Jackson behaved as if he was actually considering her theories. "I suppose it could happen," Jackson allowed. "But what I'm saying is to be vigilant. When you initially get back, you'll need to go to great lengths to make sure he avoids whatever it was that set him off and down that path he'd taken."

"I don't know all his triggers, but I do know that John

was one of them—and that, at least, won't be an issue anymore."

"Good." Why hearing that the man was out of her life had Jackson smiling to himself bothered him—but not enough for him to stop smiling. "But remember, you can't give up your own life in order for Ryan to have his. And you can't wrap him up in Bubble Wrap and watch over him 24/7. What you're shooting for," Jackson told her, "is to get to a place where you know he's watching out for himself. That he's doing the best he can for himself. He needs to grow, Debi."

She inclined her head. "Sounds good in theory," she acknowledged.

Jackson offered her his killer smile—at least that was what she had labeled it in her mind.

"Works well in practice, too," he assured her. "Keep in mind that it just doesn't happen all at once. It happens slowly, gradually. Baby steps," he emphasized for her benefit. "If you expect baby steps, then you won't be disappointed."

Miss Joan came up to their table, an old-fashioned pad and pencil in her hands. She didn't like getting away from the basics.

The smile she tendered to Jackson was one filled with affection. "I don't see you in forever and then you pop up twice in two days. I guess I have Debi to thank for this." She looked at the young woman and smiled. "Thanks for bringing Jackson around."

Debi was not one who had ever taken someone else's credit. "He brought me," Debi corrected politely.

Miss Joan didn't miss a beat. "As long as the two of you found each other here, that's all that really counts for me."

Debi had the very uneasy feeling that Miss Joan was attempting to communicate something that made precious little sense to her at the outset. The woman made it sound as if they were an item, Debi suddenly realized. Nothing could be further from her mind. For her, relationships—other than the one she had with Ryan—were all toxic. Well, she didn't have time for toxic, didn't have the time or the patience to feel her self-esteem being slowly shredded to pieces.

The old Debi wanted to be loved. This new version of her felt that love was unrealistic. The best she could hope for was to be happy if her brother could be saved.

She could live with that.

Chapter Ten

"She means well."

Debi blinked, suddenly realizing that Jackson must have said something to her, something she was apparently supposed to comment on. She'd been so lost in thought for a moment that all she had heard was a faint buzzing sound around her. She'd just assumed that it was due to the noise level in the diner.

Obviously, it wasn't.

Embarrassed, she said, "I'm sorry, what?"

"I said she means well. Miss Joan," he threw in for good measure. It occurred to him that he was trying to explain something to Debi that obviously hadn't gotten through to her. He needed to explain something else first. "Once upon a time, Miss Joan and my late uncle used to see one another on a really regular basis. That's why I think Miss Joan feels obligated to try to pair me off with someone."

"Meaning me?" Debi asked in wonder. She was an outsider. If this Miss Joan was into playing matchmaker, wouldn't the woman have picked someone she knew? Someone who lived here in this little button of a town?

But Jackson shook his head. He didn't want her to feel

intimidated. "Meaning anybody who happens to be female, unattached and within five feet of me."

"Oh."

Debi supposed she should be relieved that she wasn't giving off any particular signals that would have made the older woman think that she was fair game. Because she wasn't. Despite the fact that she was very vulnerable and lonely these days, she was determined never to put herself in that sort of a position again.

She would never allow someone else to almost literally break her heart as well as her spirit the way John had done.

In the year before her parents had been killed, she would have sworn to anyone who would have listened that she had found the kindest, most caring man on the face of the earth. Looking back, she now realized that he'd behaved that way because she had put herself at his beck and call. Time and again, she had deliberately gone out of her way to make sure that John was always happy and that if he needed something, she would fill that need for him, sometimes even before he could put that need into actual words.

In essence, without really being consciously aware of it, she had sacrificed herself, her personality and her own needs in order to make sure that John was always happy.

She only realized how much of herself she'd been giving when she had to stop giving so much of her time and effort to John. In essence, her whole life had been restructured in order to bring Ryan into her home.

Shortly after that, the kindest man in the world turned into a moody, self-centered narcissist. And he only got worse with each week that passed. As a result, she became more and more stressed.

Until the final straw came with his ultimatum.

Nope, she would never be in that kind of position again, Debi promised herself for the umpteenth time since her marriage had dissolved right in front of her like a wet tissue.

And if she was feeling more than a little attracted to the man sitting across from her, well, there were all sorts of psychological reasons for that which didn't revolve around the fact that he was probably the handsomest, sexiest man she had ever seen up close and personal.

She was just feeling sorry for herself. She'd been part of a couple for so long, it was hard for her to get used to being single again.

"Why would Miss Joan feel she had to do that?" Debi asked him after a waitress had come to take their orders and then retreated. "I mean, I'm sure that you can have your pick of willing women." Did that come out right? she silently questioned. She had a feeling that it hadn't. All she could do was hope that Jackson didn't think that she was flirting with him. "The town isn't *that* small, is it?"

Jackson watched as a faint shade of pink climbed up on her cheeks. Until this moment, he thought the idea of a woman blushing was some sort of a myth. Yet the woman he was talking to was doing just that.

Blushing.

And he found it strangely appealing.

"Not when you combine it with the number of people who are on the reservation," he acknowledged.

She'd forgotten about the reservation. About to say as much, Debi caught herself just in time. She didn't want Jackson to think she was insulting him or his heritage. It was just that the concept of a reservation was so foreign to her.

"So then, why aren't you 'spoken for'?" she asked, trying to appear as if she was asking him tongue in cheek even though part of her was genuinely curious.

Jackson shrugged carelessly. "I guess I never found the right person. That and my time's pretty much taken up with the ranch and the boys." There was another reason why he had never ventured into the marriage field. Both of his father's marriages had fallen apart because his father had cheated on one wife then just ran out on another. So, not only didn't he have a decent role model to emulate, he had his father's blood running through his veins. In his eyes, that gave him less than a fighting chance of having a decent marriage.

What was the point of trying if failure was more than just a fleeting option?

Debi thought over the excuse he'd given her. It was flimsy at best. "I'd think that the boys would probably be the ones to do whatever it is that needs doing on the ranch—and that you're one of those people who can get people to do what you want them to just by looking at them a certain way."

Now that sounded like fiction, pure and simple. Jackson laughed softly at her supposition. "You spend a lot of time reading, don't you? Escapist fiction, am I right?"

There'd been a time when she could get lost in a book. But not lately. Between her longer hours at work and her time spent either looking for Ryan or fighting with him to change his behavior, she had precious little downtime to herself.

"I don't get much of a chance to read anything these days. Work and Ryan have kept me pretty busy." Mentioning her brother brought something else to mind. She didn't like putting Jackson on the spot, but she needed to know if she was being overly optimistic about the present situation. "Full circle now, do you think he can be straightened out?"

About to answer her, Jackson saw the waitress approaching with their orders. He paused, waiting for the young woman to finish and then leave. When she did, he realized that by waiting, he had dragged the moment out for Debi. He hadn't meant to.

"I never met a boy who couldn't be straightened out," he told her.

"Is that a slogan on your brochure, or do you really believe that? Tell me honestly," she pressed, her eyes never leaving his face. Aside from being extremely handsome, he had one of those faces that weren't expressive. Thus she had no idea what he was thinking, she could only hazard a guess and then hope that she was right.

"Honestly?"

Jackson repeated the pertinent word as if he was mulling his options over. What he was actually doing was stalling, stretching out this dinner so that it lasted a little longer. He told himself it was because he was just trying to find out what sort of a life Ryan had had before coming to the ranch. But if he was being honest, he was certain that he already knew the answer to that. Although she was definitely nervous, Debi struck him as a caring person. She would have tried to make things easier on Ryan, not tougher. That's all he really needed to know about her relationship with her brother.

"Of course honestly," she responded.

He paused to take a few bites of his dinner before answering. "It's both."

"Both?" she questioned. Was she putting her faith in the wrong person after all? Her gut told her no, but then her gut would have maintained that John was a decent person she could always count on, no matter what. Look how wrong she had been there.

He explained it to her. "It's the slogan I sometimes use, but it's also something I really believe to be true. The teens who come to The Healing Ranch aren't hardened criminals or sociopaths. In most cases, they're not even terminally bad. They're just 'troubled' teens in a very real sense of the word.

"My job is to get them to think past themselves, to realize that they have a lot to give and that it's okay not to be a tough guy all the time. In order to do that, I need to find out just what caused them to want to break all the rules, to act as if a jail cell was in both their immediate and their permanent future—and to act as if they didn't care if it was.

"In Ryan's case, the reason for his behavior looks to be fairly simple." He saw the questioning look enter her eyes. He doubted if he was telling her anything that she didn't already know. Most likely, she was wondering how he had figured it out so quickly. "He blames himself for being alive."

She'd come to that conclusion herself, but each time she'd tried to approach her brother about it, Ryan shut her down, blocking any successful communication.

But she had come to that conclusion after a few months. Ryan had only been there for a couple of days. She was curious what had triggered Jackson's theory.

"Why?"

"Because there were three of them in that car that day and only he survived. Survivor's guilt is pretty common actually," Jackson told her. He found it to be rather an appalling truth. "Not that there was anything your brother could have done to prevent your parents' deaths, but that doesn't change the fact that he thinks there should have been *something* he could have done. I'm sure he's gone over the seating arrangement dozens of times in his head. Maybe if he'd sat in the front passenger seat and your mother was in the back, she'd be alive instead of him, that kind of thing."

Jackson was putting into words what had secretly been haunting her all this time, as well. To have someone else verify it, to believe that Ryan was actually going through this, just tore at her heart.

Debi stifled a helpless sigh. "You really think he thinks that way?"

Jackson nodded in response. "I'm as sure of it as I can be without having him say the actual words. But what I need to do now is to get him to open up and talk about it."

"You mean like a group therapy session?" She couldn't see that happening. She'd tried to sign Ryan up for that, but he'd refused to go. And when she literally dragged him to the psychologist's office, Ryan had shut down completely. If anything, Ryan's hostility level increased. After two attempts—and failures—she gave up trying to get him to attend the sessions.

"In a manner of speaking," Jackson allowed. The way he said it sparked her curiosity. The half smile on his lips did a little something more. "Except that in this case, the 'group' consists of horses."

"Horses?"

He nodded. "You'd be surprised what kind of things people get off their chests 'talking' to the family pet dog, or their goldfish as they're feeding it." The skeptical expression in her eyes told him she needed to be convinced. There was a time he wouldn't have believed it, either.

But Sam had showed him differently. "It's a safe way to share something that's eating away at them. After all, an animal isn't about to betray a trust and spill the secrets it was entrusted with."

"So then what?" she asked. "Do you have a recorder hidden somewhere on the horse or in the stable so you can gain some insight into the teenager you're dealing with?" She knew it was the most logical way to proceed, yet doing that seemed somehow underhanded.

She was surprised to discover that Jackson agreed with her.

He shook his head in response to her question. "Having a hidden recorder in the vicinity is just begging to destroy any sense of trust that might have been built up. That would cause more damage than good in the long run."

She hardly noticed what she was eating and did it automatically, her attention fixed on what Jackson was telling her. "So then how—?"

He liked the fact that she was questioning his procedures. So many parents would just deposit their offending offspring and wait to be called back at some future date. Ryan was a lucky kid.

"If the boy talks to his horse, that's the first step. Sharing what's weighing so heavily on them brings a sense of relief—sometimes minor, sometimes more. But letting it out—whatever 'it' is—is definitely healthy and brings with it a feeling of well-being, however minor it might be. The next time that happens, the feeling will last longer.

"In the long run, it's healing to unload the burden of whatever offense they feel they're guilty of. Sometimes it's just the offense of living when someone else isn't anymore," he told her pointedly.

That was obviously what Ryan was experiencing, she thought. "What school did you go to?" she asked, clearly impressed. When he looked at her quizzically, she added, "To get your degree in psychology."

The smile that curved his mouth created a strange, fluttery sensation within her. It left her feeling somewhat confused. Was she reacting like this because she was grateful to Jackson, or—?

"The school of hard knocks," he told her.

Was that just his modesty kicking in? "No, seriously, because you're making a lot of sense."

"Well, I'm glad that you think so," he said, finishing the last of his meal and moving the plate to one side, "but it's still the school of hard knocks."

"You didn't go to college?" she asked, surprised at the extent of his insight without any formal textbook training.

Jackson laughed shortly. "I didn't graduate high school," he confessed. "At least, not the first time around."

He had gone back to get his GED once he had decided that returning Sam's favor was going to take him in a far different direction than he had initially foreseen for himself. He'd gotten the high school diploma not to impress anyone, but to satisfy his own needs. There'd been no money for college at the time. By the time there was, he was too busy rescuing young boys' souls to take the time to go for a degree.

Debi was surprised. She came from a world where in order to accomplish anything, a person had to go to college—it was one of the things she worried about when it came to Ryan.

It was also something she and John had argued about before his ultimatum. He definitely didn't want her using "their" money to send her brother to college someday.

"Seriously?" she asked Jackson.

"It's not something I'd joke about," he replied. He looked at her empty plate. "Would you like anything else? Dessert?"

He got a kick out of the surprised look that passed over her face when she looked down at her plate and saw that it was now empty. This was a woman who could never play poker successfully, he mused. Everything was there for the world to see, right on her face.

He liked her openness, he decided. Encountering it was not an everyday occurrence.

"I'd love dessert," she confessed once she made peace with the fact that she had consumed an entire meal without even realizing it. "But I shouldn't. I don't need the extra calories."

Jackson's eyes washed over her. The woman was slender but it wouldn't take all that much to get her to look "thin"—as in skinny. "I'd say you most definitely need a few extra calories. Either that, or bricks to put in your pockets."

That didn't make any sense to her. Why would she want to carry around bricks? "Excuse me?"

"The winds kick up here every so often. Right now, I'd say that you're slender enough to blow away in a good stiff breeze." He grew serious, saying something he felt that she needed to hear. "Ryan can't afford to lose you, too."

"You twisted my arm," she conceded. She had always had a weakness for sweets. "I'll have whatever you're having."

His response was automatic. "Apple pie." Of all the various desserts that the diner offered, apple pie was a staple and also his favorite.

Her mother used to make the very best apple pies, Debi thought as a wave of nostalgia as well as sadness washed over her.

"Sounds good to me," she told Jackson.

Jackson held up his hand to get their waitress's attention. Before the young woman turned in their direction, Miss Joan saw him. In short order, she presented herself at their table.

"Everything all right?" she asked. The question appeared to be intended for both of them, but it was obvious that Miss Joan was looking pointedly at her.

Debi nodded. "Everything's very good, thank you, Miss Joan."

Miss Joan inclined her head in acknowledgment—as if she had expected nothing less.

"We'd like a couple of slices of apple pie," Jackson told the older woman.

Miss Joan glanced from one to the other. "You like the same things." There was approval in her voice. "That's good. Two pieces of apple pie, coming right up," she promised, withdrawing.

Jackson exchanged glances with Ryan's sister as Miss Joan walked to the rear of the diner. The older woman usually tried to make newcomers feel at home, but even so, Miss Joan was behaving unusually accommodating, he thought.

"Hard to believe that woman was a free-living hellion in her younger years, or so people tell me. It wasn't until she got married that she started looking at unattached people as people in search of their soul mates."

Debi thought of her own failed marriage and the dreams she'd had at the outset. She had been incredibly naive.

"I really doubt if there's any such thing as a soul mate."

The sadness in her voice had him wondering about the extent of what she had gone through. "I think Miss Joan would argue with you about that."

"She's that happy?" It wasn't that she didn't believe him, it just went against what she'd experienced. There had been a time when, if asked, she would have said that she had found her soul mate, as well.

"Yes, she is," Miss Joan said, reappearing with two servings of apple pie. She slid the two plates from the tray onto the table.

"That makes what you have very special," Debi told her, feeling somewhat awkward at being caught talking about the woman.

"I'm aware of that, honey. I'm also aware that I can't be the only one who's found someone special. The trick," Miss Joan told her, "is not to give up if you did happen to wind up with a lemon your first time out of the gate." The woman winked at her. "If you know what I mean." She smiled broadly at both of them. "Enjoy your apple pie. It's on the house."

"You can't make any money if you keep giving things away, Miss Joan," Jackson protested.

"Not just in it for the money these days. Don't need to be," she added. "Henry would turn me into a kept woman if I let him, but I like being here, watching the good people of Forever grow and evolve. Now, eat your pie and don't argue with your betters, boy," she said with a pseudo-stern expression on her face.

The next moment, Miss Joan had turned her attention to a couple seated at another table.

"Like I said earlier," Jackson said, sinking his fork into the still-warm slice of pie, "Miss Joan means well.

She does have this tendency to come on strong. But if you've got a problem, she'll be right there to help. There's nobody better to have in your corner than Miss Joan," he assured her.

"Well, with any luck, I won't be here long enough to actually *have* a corner," Debi said. And then she realized how that had to sound to him. That she was putting him on notice as to the speed she expected him to use in bringing about her brother's transformation. "No pressure," she added.

"Didn't feel any," he replied casually.

And he didn't feel pressure. For the moment, all he wanted to do was to enjoy the pie—and the company.

Chapter Eleven

He enjoyed watching the way Debi savored her dessert down to the last crumb. The look of sheer pleasure on her face made him think of total contentment.

Jackson couldn't help wondering what that was like. He'd come close, but never managed to snag that particular brass ring. To him, there was always something more that could be done, the next teen to turn around and "fix."

When Debi was done and retired her fork, Jackson looked around for Rhonda, their waitress. Spotting her, he beckoned the young woman over.

"Something else?" Rhonda asked, her glance taking in both of them.

"Just the check. For all of it," Jackson specified, indicating both Debi's order and his own by waving his index finger back and forth between them.

"But Miss Joan said not to charge you for any of it," Rhonda protested.

"What would this have cost if I *was* paying for it?" he asked.

Looking at him a little warily, the waitress did a quick tally and told him the sum. "But—"

"I know," he said, digging into his pocket and taking out his wallet, "Miss Joan said not to charge for the dinners." He extracted the amount Rhonda had mentioned, plus a good-size tip on top of that. "I pay my own way," he told the young woman.

Jackson left the waitress looking rather apprehensive as she took the hastily written-up bill and his money to the register at the front of the diner.

Jackson deliberately did *not* look in Miss Joan's direction. Instead, he held the door opened for Debi, then slipped out himself.

The night was still warm, the silken air wrapping itself around her. Debi realized that for possibly the first time in a long time, the tension that had become part of her every waking moment was missing.

Enjoy it while it lasts. Because it never lasts, she warned herself.

Turning to Jackson as they walked to his truck, she asked, "How much do I owe you?"

He took a moment before he answered. "I'll settle for a smile."

Smiles didn't pay the bills. She was fairly convinced that, based on what he was charging her for Ryan's room and board at the ranch, Jackson wasn't exactly rolling in excess cash.

She wanted to pay her fair share, even if this was an indulgence. With her temporary job at the clinic, she could breathe a little easier when it came to her available cash.

"No, really," Debi insisted.

"Really," he assured her. Coming to a stop by his vehicle, he made no move to open the door. "I'm waiting."

It took her a second to remember what he was referring to. The smile she offered came from the very center of her being. Despite the doubts she'd harbored, she'd had a nice time. Jackson was an easy person to talk to.

"You make it very hard to argue."

Her comment in turn coaxed a wide smile from him. "I've been told that."

"Like you, I'm not comfortable with not paying my own way." The man couldn't fault her for that, she thought. "How about if I work it off?" she suggested. "Maybe this weekend. I can come to the ranch, do some work for you."

"Can't think of anything that needs nursing offhand." Her work ethic was similar to his, Jackson thought. He found the thought oddly comforting.

"Then I'll do whatever it is that people do on a ranch."

Jackson cocked his head. Moonlight was beginning to tiptoe in all around them. Streaks of it wove itself through her hair, highlighting its blondness. Things began to stir within him that he had to struggle to shut down. Things he didn't want to have stirred.

"So you're offering to sit on the porch in a rocking chair and rock?" he asked teasingly.

She was prepared to work as hard as she had to. A rocking chair was not part of that plan. "Maybe after a full day's work."

Jackson looked at her knowingly. She probably hadn't realized that he'd already caught on. "You know, you don't have to go this roundabout route. You could just come straight out and ask me," he told her.

Her eyes widened, like two cornflowers turning their faces up to the sun, their source of warmth. "Ask you what?"

He could almost buy into the aura of innocence she was projecting, but she was a city girl and surviving in the big city took a certain amount of savvy. "Ask if you can come to the ranch to see Ryan."

She blew out a breath. She supposed, at bottom, that was the main reason for her being so adamant about "paying her own way."

"Am I that transparent?"

Jackson laughed. She was *utterly* transparent, but he didn't want to come out and say it so bluntly. He decided to soften the blow a little. "Well, let's just say that I wouldn't be volunteering for any spy missions if I were you."

The smile his comment roused from her was shy and all the more charming for it, Jackson thought.

"Fine, I won't." She paused for a moment, then went full steam ahead. "So it's all right? Coming to the ranch to see Ryan?"

"Sure. Go ahead. Any time." He opened the passenger door for her and held it open. "I'm not running a prison camp in the middle of Siberia." He waited as she slid in and then pulled her seat belt taut, offering it to her. "The only rule is if your brother's in the middle of doing something, wait until he's finished before taking him aside for a visit."

"Sounds reasonable," she replied.

He got in on his side, buckled up and started the engine. "That's what I always try to be," he told her. "Reasonable."

She had no idea why, since she barely knew the man, but listening to him talk made her feel that everything was going to be all right with Ryan in the long run.

Now all she needed to do was survive the short run.

HER DAYS WERE filled to the point of nearly bursting. From the moment she set foot inside the clinic until the time that she closed the door after the last of the patients finally went home, Debi felt as if she was going ninety miles an hour. Sometimes more.

At the end of the week, after the last patient of the day had left, she looked wearily at Holly. The other woman still looked relatively fresh rather than wilted, the way Debi felt.

"How can you stand it?" Debi asked.

"'It'?" Holly asked, not quite sure she understood what was being asked. She lowered the blinds, cutting off the clinic from any view of the outside world.

"The pace," Debi clarified. "It feels like we're always rushing around like crazy."

"That's probably because we are," Holly said with amusement. Moving to the coffeemaker that was set up at the rear of her reception desk, she made sure that it was off. There were times when she and the doctors ran on nothing but coffee. "And I 'stand' it because I love it. Ever since I was a little girl, all I ever wanted to be was a nurse."

She had become a surgical nurse almost by accident. It was intriguing to her to meet someone who had set their sights on the vocation right from the beginning. "A nurse, not a doctor?"

Holly shook her head. "Doctors have to be willing to leap out of bed at a moment's notice, sharp as a tack and ready to go. I'm not much good half-asleep," she confessed. "Regular hours are more my style. I get that here."

Debi could understand that. "Having regular hours is great, but it's the pace that's really killing me."

"You get used to it," she promised.

Debi had her doubts, but she didn't want to be impolite and argue the point with the other woman "If you say so."

Getting her purse out of the bottom drawer, Holly slung it over her shoulder. "Got any plans?" she asked Debi.

Debi had just retrieved her own purse. The clinic felt oddly quiet and still. She attributed it to the fact that Holly had just shut off the main lights. "Plans?" she questioned.

"For your first weekend in Forever," Holly explained. "Ray wants to have a barbecue tomorrow, invite a few friends, that kind of thing. It'll be mostly his family, but we'd love to have you." Holly's smile was warm and inviting. "A new face is always welcome."

It sounded tempting, but she had already committed herself. "Thank you for the invitation, but I'm going to have to pass on it. I already made arrangements with Jackson to come to The Healing Ranch, visit with Ryan and see how he's getting along." She realized that even as she said it, she felt her stomach tying itself up in a knot. Why? Was she afraid that Ryan wasn't doing as well as she'd hoped? Or was it something else that pricked at her nerves and caused a tingling sensation to zip right through her?

"Your brother's been on the ranch how long now?" Holly asked, trying to remember what Debi had said to her when she first came to the clinic.

"Ryan's been there a whole week. I'm not hoping for a miracle," she added quickly so Holly didn't think she was being unrealistic. "To be honest, I think it's a miracle that he hasn't taken off by now—or at least tried to."

She assumed that if that had occurred, Jackson would have notified her. But there hadn't been any communication between her and the cowboy since he'd taken her to dinner that evening. She had no idea why she kept looking over her shoulder, expecting him to just pop up. The Healing Ranch wasn't located at the end of the earth, but it wasn't exactly right on the outskirts of town, either.

"Well, I don't doubt that your brother's figured out pretty quick that there really isn't anything to run off *to* outside of Forever." Holly smiled to herself. "There's nothing but miles and miles of miles and miles."

Her brother could be pigheaded when he wanted to be. "Ryan's stubborn. If he gets it in his head to take off, he will, surrounding area be damned."

Holly frowned slightly. "Well, the area might not be, but he will if he's not careful. The weather can get downright brutally hot this time of year. Best not to go wandering off without a destination."

"Thanks for caring," she told Holly, flashing a grateful smile. "With any luck, Ryan'll come to his senses and realize that it's in his best interest to stay put, behave and do what Jackson tells him." She didn't want to think about what the alternative would mean to him—or her for that matter.

"I hope you're right," Holly said, locking the front door. "For both your sakes."

"YOU GOTTA GET me outta here," Ryan cried the moment he saw his sister coming toward him. It was ten o'clock Saturday morning and the weather was already too hot to bear. Back home he and his friends would be sneaking into an air-conditioned movie theater. Instead, he was here, sweltering in the heat. "This is nothing more than a stinking labor camp. I hope you're not paying these guys anything. They're working my tail off."

She noted that her brother wasn't cursing up a blue streak as had become his habit in the past year. She wondered if that was due to one too many encounters with the "swear jar."

Pretending to crane her neck to glimpse his rear, she said, "Your tail looks pretty intact to me."

He might not be spouting profanity, but the look in his eyes was saying censorable things. "I knew you'd take their side."

She tried to put her hand on his shoulder but he shrugged her off as if she'd just burned him. "The only side I'm on is yours."

Ryan's scowl deepened. "You sure got a hell of a way of showing it."

Okay, so maybe he hadn't been completely cured of cursing. "You're not supposed to swear, are you?" she reminded him.

If possible, he looked even more sullen than he had a moment ago. Sullen and angry. "Oh, great, now you're going to be a snitch, too?"

She was tired of tiptoeing around Ryan in order not to set him off. "Ryan, I only want what's best for you."

Ryan raised his voice, then quickly lowered it. It was obvious that he didn't want to attract any attention since it looked to him as if his sister wasn't going to rescue him the way she should. "What's best for me is getting the hell out of here and going back to Indianapolis." He looked at her plaintively. "You gotta take me!"

"Eventually," Debi agreed. "But not now—"

Frustrated anger all but radiated from every pore as Ryan accused, "He's brainwashed you. That damn cowboy brainwashed you."

She wasn't going to allow her brother to talk that way about Jackson. The man didn't deserve it. "That 'cowboy' has given me hope for the first time in a very long time."

A look of hurt betrayal passed over Ryan's face.

The next moment, he shrugged as if what his sister felt didn't matter to him. "If you're into him, fine. But don't offer me up like some kind of sacrifice just so you have something to talk about with him."

His words stung, and she struggled to convince herself that Ryan didn't mean any of it. That his low self-esteem had triggered the outburst and hurtful words.

"Ryan, I'm only going to say this once. You are here for one reason and one reason only—to turn your life around before it's too late. Now, I know you didn't steal that car, but you're a bright guy. You had to know that Wexler stole it."

Ryan's thin shoulders rose and fell in a careless, dismissive shrug. "He said it belonged to his cousin."

Ryan had to be smarter than that, she silently argued. "If it did, there was no way a relative would trust him to drive it. I wouldn't trust Wexler to drive a grocery cart down the produce aisle."

Her brother avoided her eyes, a clear sign to her that he knew she was right. "At the time it seemed okay."

"Until it wasn't," she said forcefully. "Ryan, you've got a brain in there. Please, use it."

He threw up his hands. "Fine. Great. I'll use it. I'll do anything you say—just get me out of here! Now!" he insisted.

Their voices were both raised so loud, neither one of them heard Jackson approach until he said, "Shouldn't you be getting back to work, Ryan?"

Ryan swung around, glaring at the man who was in charge. After a beat, he bent down to pick up the pitchfork he'd tossed down.

"I didn't hear you come up," Debi said, unconsciously

trying to draw his attention away from her brother until Ryan got back to work.

"It's the hay, mostly," Jackson explained. "It muffles sounds."

"Yeah, so when the bodies start dropping, you can't hear them," Ryan muttered belligerently under his breath as he went back to spreading out the hay.

Hearing him, Jackson looked far more amused than annoyed. "You found me out," he quipped. "When you finish mucking out the stalls, you get another fifteen-minute break."

Ryan merely glared at him and said nothing as he got back to work. "Yeah, right. Fine." It was hard to figure out if he was answering Jackson or just venting.

"See that?" Jackson asked her as he guided her away from where her brother was working. Ryan continued to animatedly mutter under his breath.

"See what? A surly teenager? I'm afraid I've seen way too much of that in the past couple of years or so." Ryan hadn't been like that right after the car accident, she recalled. His current behavior had evolved slowly, growing worse as time went on rather than the other way around.

"No," Jackson corrected, "what you're seeing is progress."

"Progress," she repeated. She shook her head, rather mystified. "Just how do you see that as progress?" she asked.

"The first day Ryan got here, he wouldn't budge from his bunk bed until he was told that if he didn't work, he didn't eat. He thought I was bluffing and he held out for a number of hours before he realized that I wasn't. It's amazing what a growling stomach will compel a teenager to do. Hasn't missed any work since," Jackson informed her.

"Well, that's heartening—but I think you should know, he asked me to get him out of here."

The news didn't surprise him. "I would have been suspicious if he hadn't," Jackson told her. "I've found that teenagers are a lot more prone to do something they *don't* talk about than something they keep threatening to do. It's been my experience that the ones who threaten to get involved in some sort of retaliation, for instance, generally don't do anything. They just like to talk. It's their way of knocking off steam."

She looked over her shoulder, back toward Ryan. A second teen had joined him and they seemed to be working in tandem. "Who's that?"

Jackson paused to look back. "That's Alan. He's one of the 'old-timers.'"

"Old?" she echoed, taking a closer look at the tall, thin, blond teen. "He looks like he might be all of eighteen."

"Eighteen and a half," Jackson corrected. "He first came to the ranch when he was fifteen. Like Ryan."

"And he's still here?" she questioned. Had Jackson's method failed the boy, then? Was he trying to brace her for her brother's failure down the line?

Jackson grinned. "It's not what you think. Alan successfully graduated from the program in a couple of months. I couldn't have asked for better results. But it seemed that his mother wasn't a very patient woman. She took off with her boyfriend just before Alan was set to leave here, saying that it looked to her that Alan had found a good home and should stick with it." Jackson shook his head as he thought back to the incident.

"I guess I knew something was off when her check bounced."

But the teenager was still here, Debi thought. "What did you do?"

"About the check? Wasn't very much I could do. And if you're asking about Alan, I had a choice. I could call the proper authorities and let him be absorbed by social services—and just possibly wind up in jail again—or I could take him in, have him live here on the ranch." He shrugged, downplaying the fact that, in her opinion, he just might have saved the other teenager's life. "I went with option number two."

"So you're what?" she asked, curious as to the relationship between Alan and him. "His foster parent?"

"I was until he turned eighteen. Kids automatically opt out of foster care and the system when they turn eighteen."

She glanced back toward the stable. "But he's still here."

Jackson smiled. "He likes it here and I like having him here. It all works out," he told her. "Alan's kind of the living embodiment of how the program works successfully."

Everything that Jackson was saying seemed so admirable to her. He came across as really caring about the boys who were sent here. She'd just assumed that he did it for both the money and, as Ryan had accused, for the free labor around the ranch. But after listening to Jackson, she had the feeling that this was a calling for him—and that he was aware of all the good he was accomplishing.

He was making a difference. That had to be nice.

"You know, I don't have anything planned for today and I'm sort of at loose ends. If there's anything you need doing, I'd love to pitch in." She saw a glimmer of doubt in his eyes. "I can do more than just sew up a wound and put a Band-Aid over it."

He had no doubt that she could do more, Jackson thought. A lot more.

He stopped himself. Taking that thought any further would be bringing him to a dangerous area that he had absolutely no business traversing.

But he didn't exactly want to just send her back to the hotel, either. If nothing else, being out in the fresh air was good for her—and watching her breathe, well, that was good for him on so many levels he couldn't even begin to admit to.

"Okay," he told her. "We'll put you to work. Consider yourself officially pitching in."

She smiled up at him. "I'd like that." And she didn't have to pretend she meant it, because she did. Whole-heartedly.

Chapter Twelve

"So? How's he doing?" Debi tried not to sound too anxious as she asked the question.

Ryan had been at The Healing Ranch for a little more than two weeks. To her regret, by the end of her days at the clinic, she was too tired to drive to the ranch and back in order to touch base with Jackson about her brother's progress. Today was Saturday and she was determined to make up for missed time.

Arriving at the ranch early, she looked for Jackson and was directed to the ranch house. Specifically to the cubbyholelike room that Jackson had had to turn into his office in order to keep up with the way his ranch was evolving.

Jackson put down his pen.

"The kid's coming along. We gave him his own horse to take care of. He's still trying to put up a front, complaining about the extra work, but I can tell that he's enjoying the fact that he's like everyone else now."

"His own horse?" She knew that was a badge of trust on the ranch. Debi was both happy and relieved at this turn of events. But despite what this meant, she could see that it came with its own set of problems. "That's wonderful, but is he really ready for that? I mean, the only horses Ryan's ever seen were in the movies. I don't know what he might have said, but he doesn't know how to ride one," she warned.

"Don't worry about that," Jackson told her. "Riding—and any necessary riding lessons—comes in due time. Right now, he's learning how to care for the animal, how to read signs."

"Signs?" She wasn't sure she understood what Jackson was referring to.

Jackson nodded as he leaned back in his chair. It had been Sam's favorite chair in his last few years. The subtle creak whenever he moved reminded him of his uncle and he unconsciously smiled.

"The kind that the horse gives off," he told her. "The bond between a horse and its master can be very strong if it's nurtured correctly. Ryan learns to relate to horses, then people aren't far behind."

She remembered that he'd told her that when she and Ryan had first arrived. "Sounds good to me. And just between us, it can't be happening fast enough for me."

Why that bothered him was something else he wasn't going to explore. Instead, he made the natural assumption. "Anxious to leave our tiny dot of a town?"

The question surprised her. She hadn't realized that her statement could be taken that way. "Actually, no, I'm beginning to like it here."

He looked at her quizzically. She had lost him. "Then why…?"

She was, for the most part, a private person. But she felt as if she knew this man who was working miracles in her life. And at this point, she could admit to herself that she needed to be able to share the parameters of her situation with someone. Jackson seemed like the natural choice.

"Things are getting a little tight," she confessed. "I'm running low on funds even with the job you got me at the clinic."

"I didn't get you the job," Jackson corrected. "I just brought you to the clinic. *You* got you the job." He paused a moment, carefully thinking through what he was about to say next. "You know, not to take anything away from the town's new hotel, but we've got a spare bedroom here at the ranch. You're welcome to stay in it until your brother completes his course here."

Not having to pay for the hotel room for another two to four weeks would be a huge help. But then again, she felt as if she was taking unfair advantage of Jackson's generosity.

"I can't impose on you like that," she protested.

"*Imposing* is if you declared you were moving in without first being invited to do it," Jackson pointed out even as a small voice in his head whispered that he was asking for trouble. He deliberately ignored it. "You're not imposing."

She still didn't feel right about this. "But Garrett lives here, too, right? Won't my staying at the ranch house bother him?"

Jackson laughed softly. "Garrett's the easygoing one in the family. And it would be nice to hear a female voice once in a while, so you'd actually be doing us a favor by staying here."

She readily admitted that there were areas she was still naive about, but this was taking it to an extreme. She did, however, appreciate what he was trying to do. "And if I believe that, there's a bridge you want to sell me, right?"

"Fresh out of bridges," he told her. "But I still have that bedroom."

Debi looked at him, debating, and sorely tempted to take the man up on his offer. It would solve her most immediate problem.

It took her less than two minutes to resolve her internal argument. She nodded, accepting his generous offer. This way, though she'd have to drive back and forth for the job at the clinic, she'd get a chance to be close by for Ryan, which was, after all, the entire reason she had remained in this town in the first place.

And maybe, just maybe, her proximity might even speed his progress along. She just needed to know one thing. "How much?"

"How much?" Jackson echoed quizzically.

"Yes. The bedroom," she specified. "How much is it per week?" She imagined that would be the best way to go since she wasn't sure how long it would take to bring Ryan completely around, back to the caring, sensitive and intelligent person he had once been.

"Well, I don't really know," Jackson replied, his expression entirely emotionless, "but when I figure out what bedrooms are going for, I'll let you know."

"Very funny. I meant how much rent would I be paying for the bedroom?"

He'd been like her once, suspicious and wary of any offer of kindness. In a way, there were a lot of similarities between Debi and the boys in terms of what they were all going through. And because he could remember and relate, that gave him the confidence that came with knowing that the situation could be reversed. Not easily, but definitely with effort.

"You wouldn't be," he answered. "I'm offering you

the room for the duration of your stay in Forever free of charge."

"Why?" He didn't really know her. She'd been a stranger less than a month ago, before she'd gotten in contact with him about his program. Why would he take a stranger into his house?

"Because it might help Ryan to know that you're somewhere on the premises. I think he feels that you have his back."

"He certainly doesn't act like it. The last time I talked to him, he sounded angry because I wasn't springing him and taking him home."

"Trust me. He's glad you're here and having you that much closer might just help him."

"Well, I know it would help me," she freely admitted to Jackson.

He didn't need to hear any more. "Then it's settled. I'll have the room ready for you by the time you get back from the hotel with your things."

This hunk of a cowboy was an answer to a prayer, she thought. Not only was Jackson making headway with Ryan when she couldn't, but he'd just found a way to keep her from slipping into a Chapter 11 situation. Between paying a lawyer to handle her divorce and paying for Ryan's stay here, her small life savings had been wiped out.

For that matter, she wasn't even sure if the position at the hospital that she had taken a hiatus from would still be there waiting for her when she got back. They'd said they'd hold it for her, but times were tough and situations changed. To know that she would have a little something to tide her and Ryan over until she could find another job was at least comforting to some extent.

"You're serious?" she asked, scrutinizing his face just to be sure.

To reassure Debi, he smiled as he said, "Completely." It was impulse that had her all but chattering as she thanked him profusely. And impulse was also to blame for what she caught herself doing next.

She had no memory of thinking this through. On the contrary, all she remembered, after the fact, was that one second she felt a huge sense of relief and joy surging through her, the next, she found her arms around the back of Jackson's neck and her lips directly on his.

It was supposed to be a spontaneous kiss between friends to say thank-you.

It was supposed to be just a quick, uncomplicated kiss with a life span of a second.

Maybe two.

It turned out to be, and say, a whole lot more than that.

First contact told her she was getting much more than she had bargained for.

He made her blood rush and her heart pound hard, the way it did when she poured it on for the last quarter mile of a run.

But a run had never made her head spin.

Jackson did.

The man's kiss packed a punch she wasn't prepared for. Until just now, she considered herself well-versed in the world of male/female relations. But now she realized that she was just a novice. Nothing she had *ever* experienced with John held a candle to what had just happened here with Jackson.

Certainly she'd never felt this kind of fire erupting within her.

He knew he should stop.

Knew he shouldn't have even allowed it to happen in the first place. But she had managed to catch him by surprise. In more ways than one. The second she'd thrown her arms around his neck, he'd known what was coming.

Or thought he did.

For a little thing, she could really bring him down to his knees. As it was, the aforementioned knees felt rather unstable for a moment or two, like they could collapse at any second.

This was a compromising situation, one he didn't want any of the teens on the ranch to be aware of. Luckily, when he'd checked recently, they were all in the corral. To the best of his knowledge, no one had witnessed what had just transpired. But he still didn't believe in taking chances.

And he was going to put a stop to this…any second now.

The truth of it was, he found himself enjoying this intimate contact far more than he thought he would.

Far more than he should.

And yet, there was no denying that it—and she—were having one hell of a dynamic effect on him.

Debi stepped back first.

"I wanted to thank you," she told him with feeling.

"I think you just did," Jackson responded. Pulling himself together, he made a suggestion, not realizing that he'd already said the same thing until the words were out of his mouth. That kiss had temporarily scrambled his brain. "Why don't you go back to the hotel, check out and come back with your things? After that, if you're still bent on helping with the chores—"

"I am," she told him eagerly. "Now more than ever." If he wasn't going to take money for the room, then she *had* to do something around the ranch that could be seen as payment.

"—I'll make up a list for you, if you insist," he said. "But just so you know, while the boys all have to pull their own weight around here, that doesn't apply to you. You've already got a full-time job. As far as I'm concerned, you're a guest here, which means that you don't have to do anything."

"I've never known how to do nothing," she confided.

"Well, you certainly can't be accused of doing nothing, not when you're working at the clinic. The way I see it, every hour there is equal to at least two hours in the real world. I'd think that it would leave you pretty exhausted."

"It did, but I've had a full night's sleep to recharge," she told him. "I feel pretty energetic, so your wish is my command."

His eyes drew together as he tried to remember something. "That's from a fairy tale, right?"

"Even fairy tales are based on a grain of truth," she reminded him.

Looking at her now, standing on the other side of his desk, he really felt as if he was in a fairy tale. The troubled kid he had once been could have never foreseen his life evolving this way.

I owe you, Sam. Big time, Jackson thought.

"Want me to drive you to the hotel?" he offered out loud.

"No, that's okay. I definitely know the way back. I'll be fine," she assured him. "You go do your ranching things," Debi said, her words deliberately vague since she really didn't know what needed doing on this sort of a ranch. "I'll try to be back as fast as I can," she promised.

"You don't have to hurry," he told her, moving back

behind his desk and sitting down again. "The room's not going to go anywhere."

He was making her feel safe, she realized. There was a danger in that. She'd let her guard down at some point and then that would leave her wide-open and vulnerable. She couldn't allow that to happen.

And yet, there was something almost seductive about not having to worry, about feeling protected and safe.

She was just deluding herself, Debi silently insisted. Squaring her shoulders, she replied, "You never know. Someone might make you a better offer than getting nothing for your trouble."

"Not everything comes down to a matter of dollars and cents," he told her. Picking up his pen again, he said, "See you later," and got back to work.

HE WASN'T AWARE of Garrett immediately.

Debi had hurried off and he forced himself to return to the part of running The Healing Ranch that he hated: filling out reports, keeping logs. He managed to cope with it because he knew that there was no way around the requirement. The sooner he got to the monthly endeavor, the sooner he would be done with it and free.

He'd made his peace with the fact that the reports were a necessary evil.

Somewhere into this storm of papers and recently released hormones running rampant through his system his brother walked into the office.

Jackson had no idea how long Garrett had stood there, in the rear doorway, observing him. All he knew was that he'd started to sense his brother's presence. Looking up, he saw that Garrett had on that strange, bemused expression that he sometimes sported.

He was also grinning.

From ear to ear.

"What?" he asked when he and Garrett made eye contact.

Garrett merely shrugged, dismissing the question. "Nothing." The grin, however, remained. If possible, it grew even wider.

"Nothing my eye," Jackson retorted. He didn't feel like playing games. "Out with it. You don't grin like that over nothing," he maintained.

Jackson had the uneasy feeling that maybe he and Debi hadn't gone unobserved after all. How long had Garrett been standing there?

Coming all the way into the room, Garrett perched for a moment on the edge of the desk. His brother pointedly looked into his eyes. "I was just beginning to get used to the idea that I was never going to see you attracted to anyone."

"And you still haven't," Jackson replied curtly.

"Okay," Garrett allowed. "Then I hate to tell you this, Jackson, but you have a perfect clone and he's alive and well and practically living right on top of you—or at least in your shadow."

"What are you doing here, anyway? Aren't you supposed to be out at the corral?"

"I just came in to get a book." Moving over to the narrow bookcase, he extracted a worn book that had once belonged to their uncle. It contained illustrations of all the different breeds of horses that existed.

"Well, you got it. You can go now," Jackson told him dismissively. He deliberately looked back down at the reports he was filling out.

"Okay" Garrett began to take his leave, then turned

around for one last word. "Don't get me wrong, it's really nice to see a spring in your step. That means—I think—that you're not selling Ryan on the idea of leaving, say, within the next week."

"You know better than that," Jackson replied. "If he stays, it's because he might need a little more work before he can be put back into the so-called general population—otherwise known as everyday society," Jackson told his brother. "It's nothing personal."

Garrett grinned, something he was far more given to doing than his older brother. "Of course it's not."

Rising from behind his desk, Jackson crossed to the open doorway and looked around. There was no one there. This time. Closing the door, he turned his attention back to his brother.

"Garrett, you know we both take this job seriously. If someone had just overheard your tone, they might take things the wrong way and that just might undermine all the good we're doing here."

Garrett dismissed the idea with a wave of his hand. "All anyone has to do is call on any one of the 'ranch hands' who got through this 'course.' They'll see the good you've done."

"*We've* done," Jackson corrected him.

But Garrett shook his head. "I was right the first time. I'm just following your lead, big brother. You're the one who decided to do this after Sam died. I guess everything happens for a reason," he continued. "If you hadn't been such a big screw-up, Mom wouldn't have called on Sam to come help her and we would have never inherited this ranch."

Jackson sincerely doubted that. "He had no next of kin, remember?"

"He had Dad," his brother reminded him, his own smile fading.

Neither one of them had good memories of the man even before he'd walked out on them. "That's taking it for granted that our illustrious father is still alive somewhere. Just between you and me, I don't think his kidneys could have held on for very long. The man went through booze like other people go through water."

Garrett didn't realize that he'd winced. "He was a mean drunk."

Jackson laughed shortly. His eyes were somber. "He wasn't exactly a walk in the park when he was sober, either," he recalled. Years ago he'd come to the conclusion that in their case, they were far better off with an absentee father than living under the same roof with someone who was volatile, unpredictable and lashed out with his fists without any warning.

Garrett nodded. Opening the door, he started to go when something occurred to him. "Oh, and Jackson?"

He was never going to finish wading through this annoying paperwork, he thought, looking up. "Yeah?"

"She's a honey. The girl I saw you lip-locking with. Ryan's sister, right?" he recalled, although her name escaped him at the moment. "She's a honey."

Jackson blew out a breath. Served him right for giving in to a flash of desire. "Spare me the fifty-cent analysis and get back to work like the helpful brother you're not being."

"I'll get right on it," Garrett said perhaps a bit too quickly in his estimation. "Oh, and when the big day comes—"

"*What* big day?" Jackson demanded, confused. What was Garrett babbling about?

"*The* big day," Garrett repeated with more emphasis. The look he gave his brother clearly said that he should know what the reference was regarding. "Just remember, I get dibs on best man."

"If I find a best man," Jackson deadpanned, putting a literal meaning to his brother's words, "I'll be sure to send him along to you."

He ducked his head as Garrett threw the book he'd come for at him.

Chapter Thirteen

"Hey Debs, I bet you never thought you'd ever see me doing this!" Ryan called out to her in a loud voice.

Debi's heart swelled. He sounded excited, just the way he used to before that horrendous car accident had changed everything.

She silently blessed Jackson before she even turned toward the sound of Ryan's voice. Any change for the better with Ryan was because of him and the man had earned her undying gratitude.

Another two weeks had passed.

Two weeks during which time she drove into town in the morning and back to the ranch at the end of her day. Two weeks of a routine that she was surprised to discover herself liking more and more.

Who would have ever thought that was possible? Certainly not her.

Another surprise was that she was becoming entrenched in this low-key town life. Her transformation was happening so easily, so effortlessly, it all but took her breath away.

Because of the steady and usually heavy traffic of people through the clinic, she was getting acquainted with a great many of Forever's citizens. Some of whom

had taken to bringing her things—cookies, fudge, a cro-
cheted poncho—to either say thank-you to her, or in some
cases "welcome to Forever."

To the latter group, she tried to gently but tactfully explain that she wasn't planning on staying, but they would
look at her with knowing looks and just smile. Eventually, she gave up. They would realize the truth once she
was gone, she decided.

She had no idea why that thought brought a strange
tinge of sorrow with it.

And following her routine, when she came home at
night—and The Healing Ranch *had* become home to
her—she became part of that life, as well.

Maybe even more so.

The teenagers in Jackson and Garrett's care ate dinner at the house every night and Jackson made sure that
there was always a place set for her.

The first night she'd come to the ranch, thinking that
she would just quietly slip in and go to the room he'd set
aside for her, Jackson had derailed her plan. He'd been
waiting for her on the front porch. The moment she'd arrived, Jackson had taken her by the hand and drawn her
into the dining room.

"I'm thinking you haven't had dinner yet," he had
said to her.

Which was when she'd held up the bag she'd picked
up on her way back. "I picked up something to go at the
diner," she'd explained.

Jackson had paused to take the bag from her, saying,
"It can just 'go' to the refrigerator. Don't worry, it won't
go to waste. You can have it for lunch tomorrow."

Gesturing toward the empty chair remaining, he'd
coaxed, "Why don't you sit down?"

Even with all those faces turned toward her, watching her intently, Debi was still going to beg off, thinking that she'd feel awkward eating in their midst and that Jackson was only asking her to join them because he felt sorry for her.

But then she saw that Ryan was sitting just two seats down. He said nothing, but the look in his eyes asked her to stay.

That was enough for her.

Offering Jackson and Garrett a smile, she said, "Okay," and sank down into the chair.

That had been her first step in becoming part of The Healing Ranch's daily life.

In an odd way, the ranch did as much healing for her as it was supposed to be doing for all the troubled teens who had been sent here by desperate parents and relatives in hopes of bringing about some kind of miraculous transformation.

Every night she hurried home for dinner a little more quickly than the last, a sense of anticipation spurring her on. Having parked her car a ways from the ranch house, she was quickly walking toward it, passing by the corral on her way.

That was when she heard Ryan calling out to her. Happy that the sullen tone was absent from his voice, she turned to look in his direction. Her mouth dropped open.

She hardly remembered cutting across the rest of the distance. All she was aware of was smiling at him, broadly. *Yes, Debi, there is a Santa Claus*, she thought to herself. Had Jackson been there, she would have kissed him. The spark was returning into Ryan's eyes.

"You're right about that," she answered. Ryan was sitting in a saddle, astride a beautiful palomino. "You look like a natural," she told him.

Out of the corner of her eye, she saw that Garrett and Alan, the teen who Jackson had taken into his home, were both mounted on their horses, as well, and though they were good at masking what they were about, they were both paying very close attention to her brother.

"Wanna see me jump Jericho?" Ryan asked her eagerly, his body language indicating that he was all set to act on his offer.

"Isn't it almost dinnertime?" she asked, avoiding commenting directly on her brother's question. "Shouldn't you be getting ready?"

"She's right, Ry," Garrett told him. "Time to put our horses away."

Ryan appeared somewhat crestfallen, and she fully expected him to argue with Garrett. When he didn't, she was stunned.

Progress! Debi thought triumphantly. Three weeks ago, her brother would have argued, hurled curse words and pouted until he got Garrett to give in—or, more likely, was sent to the bunkhouse without dinner. This new, respectful Ryan restored her hope for the future.

Maybe by the time this was all over, she *would* have the old Ryan back. Permanently.

It was something to hope for.

"Someone certainly looks like she's happy," Jackson commented. Entering the living room, he caught the look on her face as she walked into the house.

The word *happy* didn't even begin to cover the way she felt. Seeing Ryan behaving like his old self filled her with a euphoric high that was almost dizzying.

Before she could think through her next action, Debi

crossed over to the man she held responsible for her brother's metamorphosis, braced her hands on his shoulders, raised herself up on her toes and brushed her lips against his cheek. "Someone is *very* happy," she told him.

The feel of her lips fleetingly brushing against his skin stirred an entire cauldron of dormant emotions that were simmering just beneath the surface, awakening a longing within him that he hadn't even known was there. It took effort to stop himself from just taking her into his arms and kissing her back.

Really kissing her.

He did his best to hide his feelings as he asked, "Good day at the clinic?"

"The day at the clinic was good," she confirmed, then added, "But this evening at the ranch is positively great." When Jackson cocked his head slightly as if waiting for an explanation, she filled in the blanks. "I just saw Ryan *riding* his horse. He looked happier than I've seen him in a long, long time." She blinked back tears of joy. She'd all but given up hope that Ryan could be reached this way. "When did he learn how to ride?"

"It's an ongoing thing," Jackson told her matter-of-factly. "I mean, what's the point in having a horse if you can't ride it, right?" He paused, as if deciding whether or not to say anything. And then he did. "You're crying. Are you upset?"

She shook her head. "No, I'm happy."

Digging into his back pocket, he took out a handkerchief and offered it to her. "I'll *never* understand women," he freely confessed.

She wiped away the tearstains on her cheeks, then handed the handkerchief back to him.

"This is like a miracle. Ryan never showed much interest in animals. Never begged for a pet dog or anything like that. Now it looks like your brother's going to have to all but peel him out of the saddle." She glanced over her shoulder toward where the corral would have been if there was no ranch house separating her from the view. She caught her bottom lip between her teeth for a moment, thinking. "Maybe Garrett needs my help." Saying that, she did an about-face in the living room, and began heading for the front door.

Jackson caught up to her in two strides and took hold of her arm, stopping her. "Stop worrying," he told her. "Garrett knows how to handle the situation. Ryan will be okay."

"I'm not worried about Ryan, I'm concerned about Garrett," she confessed.

That amused him, given that his brother was six-one with a body built by ranching and her brother was around five-ten and might tip the scales at one thirty-five if he carried rocks in his pockets.

"My brother hasn't met a boy he couldn't get along with. Stop worrying," Jackson repeated. "Go back to being happy," he coaxed. "It looks good on you."

Jackson was right, she thought. She had to back away and let things play themselves out.

Hanging up her purse on the coatrack by the door, she followed Jackson into the kitchen.

"Need any help with dinner?" she offered. The next moment, she felt it was only fair to tell him how limited her abilities in the kitchen were. "I can stir ingredients with the best of them."

"Not necessary," he told her. "Everything's all under control." Grabbing two towels, one in each hand, Jackson opened the oven door and slid out the pan of pork tenderloin that was to be the main course. "Ryan, by the way, is a natural. I watched him earlier in the corral," he explained. "You never took him horseback riding?"

Debi shook her head, then brushed away the hair that insisted on falling into her eyes. "Not even on one of those things that gives you a three-minute ride if you feed it enough quarters."

"How about you?" he asked. "Did you ever ride a horse?"

She didn't see the connection, but she answered, "Not too many occasions for that in the city. There aren't exactly a lot of horses wandering around Indianapolis."

"There are stables around if you know where to look for them," he told her, placing the pan on top of the counter. "They might not be smack-dab in the middle of the city, but they're around." He shut off the oven, then turned off the vegetables that were being cooked on top of the stove. "Not interested in riding?" he asked.

She hadn't really thought about it one way or another—until just now. "No, it's just not something I ever got around to. But I wouldn't mind learning someday."

The corners of his mouth curved ever so slightly. "Someday," he repeated.

"Uh-huh. Someday." Debi wanted to do *something*, be useful in order to show him her gratitude. She glanced into the dining room. The dishes weren't out yet. "Let me set the table for you," she offered.

Not waiting for Jackson's response, she went into the cupboard and began taking down the necessary plates and glasses as well as gathering the utensils out of the drawers.

Watching her, Jackson smiled to himself. "Why don't you do that?" he agreed as he went to strain the vegetables.

THE TENDERLOIN ALL but melted in her mouth. She was quickly coming to the conclusion that there was *nothing* that Jackson White Eagle couldn't do once he set his mind to it.

The boys at the table polished off both the tenderloin and the generous servings of corn, carrots and mashed potatoes that had been placed beside the main course. Fresh air and the day's work gave them all healthy appetites.

When the meal was over, Debi rose from the table and began clearing away the dishes. She might not be any help when it came to the actual cooking, but she at least knew how to clean.

But as she turned with a stack of dinner plates in her hands, Jackson put himself in front of her. Before she could say a word, Jackson took the dishes from her. The next moment, he turned to the first teen seated at his right. "Jim, you and Gabe take care of these for me. Nathan, you've got the glasses. Jerry, the knives and forks. Ryan, you've got the serving plates. That leaves the pots and pans to you three," he said, addressing the last three teens in his care.

"They can't all be at the sink at the same time," Alan pointed out.

"Work it out," Jackson instructed in a tone that told the boys he knew they would.

Debi frowned as she saw the teens complying immediately. She wasn't accustomed to just standing back and letting someone else do all the work. In this instance, several someones.

"I can do that," she protested to Jackson.

"Right now, you're going to be busy dealing with

something else," Jackson told her. Placing his hand to the small of her back, he guided her out of the dining room.

"I don't understand," she told him.

"Easy," he explained as they reached the front door. "'Someday' is here."

Okay, now he had really lost her. "What?"

He paused right outside the front door. "You said that you'd like to learn how to ride someday. You're going to need someone to teach you. I'm volunteering, which means that 'someday' is here."

She looked at him uncertainly. Her uncertainty increased as he laced his fingers through hers and ushered her off to the stables.

"Wait, I didn't mean that I wanted to learn immediately."

"That's good, because you don't learn how to ride immediately. You learn how to ride slowly, in stages," he outlined as they arrived at the stables. "Today," he told her as they walked inside, "we're just going to get you to mount a horse."

"Right after dinner?" she asked nervously.

"Riding a horse is not like swimming," Jackson informed her with a laugh. "And anyway, you're not going to be riding tonight. I just want to get you comfortable *sitting* on a horse."

Suddenly, the animals that were in the stalls looked prohibitively large to her. Larger than they had an hour ago. She didn't know about this.

"If you really want me to be comfortable," she told him, "maybe we should start out with a rocking horse."

Jackson thought he heard a quaver in her voice. "Debi, are you afraid of horses?" he asked her.

"No," she protested instantly, then, flushing, she reversed her statement. "Yes." But that wasn't the answer she wanted to settle on because what she was feeling was complicated. "I mean— Well, maybe. I guess I'm not quite sure yet."

This wasn't some kind of deep-seated fear caused by a traumatic incident in her childhood. He saw none of that in her eyes and was convinced that had there been something like that in her past, he would have been able to pick up on at least some of the signs. There were none.

Which meant he was free to proceed in making her come around.

"Come here," he requested. When she did, albeit somewhat hesitantly, he took her by the hand and drew her closer to the horse in the stall. "This is Annabelle," he told her. "She's the gentlest horse on the ranch. Why don't you try petting her?" he suggested.

"You're sure it's all right?" she asked. "I mean, it won't bother her?"

"None of the animals feel threatened if they're petted," Jackson promised her seriously. "Most animals don't," he added, looking at her significantly.

When she still hesitated, Jackson took her hand, cupped his own over it and then brought it up to the mare's muzzle. He then went on to slowly pass her hand over Annabelle.

"Do it just like this," he urged as he guided her through the motions. He could almost see her heart pounding in her throat. "See how easy it is?" he asked quietly, soothingly.

She had to admit that the muzzle felt almost silky beneath her fingers. The longer she stroked the mare, the more she found that she enjoyed the contact.

"I'm just a little worried that she might be too tired," she told Jackson.

"Just for the record," he told her, tongue in cheek, "I've never met an animal who was too tired to be petted. As a matter of fact, they perk up when you do that. Keep it up," he urged.

Taking his hand away from hers, he reached into his back pocket. Finding what he was looking for, he extended his hand out and opened it. There were a couple of lumps of sugar in his palm.

"Here, give her these."

Taking the lumps of sugar from him, Debi looked down at them, and then raised her eyes to his. "Are we bribing her?"

"Yes, we are. Bribing her to like you," Jackson explained, then added in a slightly lower voice, "Not that that's actually necessary. I doubt if anyone, man or beast, ever had to be bribed to like you," he said, momentarily thinking back to her enthusiastic kiss that first evening she had joined his household. It felt as if it had only happened a moment ago—and yet, at the same time it seemed so far in the past. Having her brush her lips against his cheek earlier had just stirred up his reaction to her.

Jackson shook himself free of the memory, but not nearly as quickly as he would have liked to or felt that he should have.

It also didn't help that while the memory had flashed through his mind, he had savored it.

"When do I get to ride her?" Debi asked.

"Maybe in a few days." Jackson didn't want to rush things. Given her extreme inexperience, there was a risk of Debi possibly falling off and getting hurt. He didn't want to take that chance.

"A few days?" she echoed in surprise—and disappointment. "I have to wait that long?"

"It's not that long," he assured her. But she didn't look convinced. "Like I said, we take this all very slowly, a little bit at a time. You master one step, we go on to another," he promised.

She rested her hand on the mare's muzzle. "And what am I mastering now?"

Jackson grinned, his blue eyes crinkling. "That's easy," he told her. "Petting."

Green eyes met blue. "I think that I've got that part down pat at this point," she told him quietly.

"Great." Jackson nodded his head, more to himself than to her. "Tomorrow you get to lead your horse around the perimeter of the corral."

"Is that when I get to ride her?" she asked, hoping for the green light.

Obviously she had missed the word *lead*, he thought. "No, you get to walk right alongside of her while *she's* walking, hence the word *lead*."

She didn't quite understand why she'd be walking around the perimeter of the corral, holding on to the horse.

"Are we going to be looking for something?" she asked.

"Yes," he replied. "Patience. To be a good rider, you have to have patience. Patience to build up a relationship with the horse."

"I don't want to marry the horse, I just want to ride her," she protested.

He watched her for a long moment. She was almost pouting. Jackson had to admit that it got under his skin, but not in an irritating sort of way. That was happening far too often It was just unsettling enough to cause what amounted to upheavals in places that were better left unaffected and alone. He could afford to have feelings for Debi.

Too late for that, Jackson thought.

What he needed was a battle plan. One where he could come out the victor.

The next second, he realized that was *not* going to be as easy as it might sound.

Chapter Fourteen

Jackson thought over his options. He wanted to keep Debi safe, but he didn't want to do it by shutting down her spirit. He came up with a compromise.

He thought it was a good compromise, but then, he *was* the one who had come up with it.

"Okay, tell you what. There is a way that I can let you get up on that horse tonight."

She looked at him for a long moment and realized that she trusted him. Maybe that was naive of her, especially after what had happened with the last man she had trusted—John had made her doubt herself and everything she had ever believed in.

But there was something honest—for lack of a better word—about Jackson, something that told her he had her best interests at heart because he had *everyone's* best interests at heart.

"Okay, I'm listening," she said, gamely waiting for him to tell her the terms he had come up with.

"You can get into Annabelle's saddle, but I'm going to be the one holding on to the reins and leading you around the corral." He looked at Debi to gauge her response to his idea.

"You mean like a pony ride in an amusement park?"

She could almost envision it. To her mind, the whole thing seemed painfully ludicrous.

Thinking it over, Jackson inclined his head. "In a way, I guess you hit it dead-on. Yes, like a pony ride in an amusement park—except a lot quieter because the other kids won't be around."

They obviously had different opinions of pony rides and amusement parks. Being taken to one--which he never had—symbolized caring parents and a happy childhood—something else he'd also never had.

His eyes met hers. He could see Debi's natural resistance. He sensed that she liked being independent and that was all well and good, except that wasn't going to work in this particular situation.

"It's the only way," he informed her, his voice quiet but nonetheless firm. The last thing he wanted was for her to get hurt. Annabelle was gentle, but like any horse, she could be spooked. He wasn't about to take chances. His reason for that went far beyond not wanting his insurance premiums to rise.

"I'd feel like a kid," Debi protested. She was a grown woman, which meant she could hold her own reins. Or rather the horse's, she silently amended.

"No, you wouldn't," Jackson corrected. "Because all the kids at The Healing Ranch have to show that they can master every step before they can move on to the next step. An inexperienced novice to the sport wouldn't ask to leap from being that to riding like a moderately experienced horsewoman in one step," he pointed out. Jackson crossed his arms before him and studied her face. "Now, what'll it be?"

Debi knew there was only one answer she *could* give him. Otherwise, she had a very strong feeling that her horseback experience would be put on hold, maybe even indefinitely.

Still, she wasn't above trying to persuade him to see it her way at least once.

"Tell you what, I'll do it the right way starting tomorrow evening—if I can ride Annabelle on my own for five minutes tonight." She followed up the proposition with a wide, hopeful smile. "Please?"

Jackson ignored her smile—for her own good. It wasn't exactly easy, but then, he could be stoic when he had to be.

"My way," he reminded her.

Her smile vanished, replaced by a frustrated frown. "You're being overly cautious."

Maybe he was, but it was far better to be safe than to be sorry. He knew what the latter could feel like. "My way."

Debi blew out a breath, fairly convinced that there was no way she was going to change his mind. She might as well give up gracefully.

"Your way," she said with a quick bob of her head as she conceded the point—and game—to him.

To her surprise, Jackson didn't gloat or look smug for having won, the way she'd expected. Instead, he merely nodded and immediately got started. "Okay, let me show you where we keep the saddles and the rest of the gear you'll need."

She followed right on his heel to the closet. When he opened the doors, she saw that there were stacks of saddles, blankets and bridles.

Collecting what was needed, Jackson proceeded to demonstrate to her the proper way to saddle a horse. Debi watched, making mental notes for when he had her do it—as she was completely certain that he would. Jackson led by example—but he expected that example to be closely followed to the letter.

"Wait, doesn't that hurt her?" Debi asked, concerned, when she saw Jackson start to put the bridle bit into the mare's mouth.

Quite honestly, she had never given what was involved in preparing a horse to be ridden any thought one way or the other. But being so close to the animal as it was taking place made Debi so much more aware of the process.

"They fight against it at first, but not because having the bit in their mouths hurts. They fight it because they instinctively know that it means the intended rider is exercising dominance over them. The horses resist that at all costs in the beginning. It's only natural," he emphasized. He saw the way Debi was eyeing Annabelle and guessed at what was going on in her head. "She's used to me, that's why she doesn't fight anything I do. She trusts me," he added proudly. "For the most part, once a horse is broken in, they pretty much put up with being bridled and saddled without a fuss—unless whoever's doing it mishandles them or treats them cruelly."

Finished, Jackson took hold of the bridle with one hand, holding on to it lightly.

"Ready?" he asked Debi.

She was a little nervous, but Ryan had done this, she told herself. If he could do it, then she could. After all, she was the older sibling, not Ryan. And as the big sister, she had an obligation to always be the one whom Ryan looked up to, the one who would always be an example for him to model himself after. That meant jumping into the deep end of the pool even if all she had was one swim ming lesson under her belt. She had to be fearless so that her brother would never entertain fear.

She had to be good so that he didn't fail. There it was, all tied up in a bow. The philosophy that helmed her life.

"I was born ready," she answered him.

Jackson tried not to smile at that. Just as he tried not to smile as he watched her attempt to put her foot into the stirrup and mount Annabelle.

And fail.

Then fail again.

"Would you like a little boost?" he finally suggested after her third unsuccessful attempt to swing herself into the saddle.

Debi hated admitting defeat. "How do the boys do it?" she asked, frustrated.

"Simple. They're taller than you. And they're used to this. Now, about that help?" he asked her, waiting.

At least he didn't say the teens were more agile than she was. Looking back at Jackson, she knew she wasn't going to get any help from him until she officially asked him for it. Resigned, she gave in.

"Yes, please," she said grudgingly, wary about just what that so-called "help" from Jackson might ultimately wind up being.

To her surprise, Jackson stood before her, laced his fingers together and then bent down, holding his interlaced hands right in front of her.

The implication was clear, but when she continued to just stare at his hands, Jackson spoke up to encourage her.

"Go ahead, put your foot right here." To move things along, Jackson bent down even farther so that she could easily comply with his directions. "Grab hold of the saddle horn with one hand so that you can pull yourself up.

Meanwhile, put your foot right here in my hands," he instructed again.

Feeling a little strange, not to mention rather wobbly, Debi did as she was told. Liftoff was less than smooth, but she did manage it, which was all that counted.

"Hey, it worked," she cried happily.

"Yeah, how about that." Jackson pretended to be just as surprised as she was. He secretly enjoyed this display of enthusiasm he saw.

Taking the reins in his hand, he proceeded to lead her horse out of the stables and into the corral.

"Hold on to the saddle horn," he advised.

"Again?" While happy, she still wanted reasons for everything. "Why?"

"So you don't fall off," he answered simply.

"I *do* have a sense of balance, you know," she protested, then added, "You know, you worry too much."

"Keeps my insurance premiums down," he quipped without looking over his shoulder at her. He just continued walking as he led her horse in a circle.

She hadn't thought of that. Just because this was a rural area of the country and he was running a ranch didn't mean that they were separated from all the annoying, so-called finer points of civilization. Like needing insurance for protection against circumstances that could bring about the loss of the ranch.

After all, Jackson ran a ranch that took in troubled teens. Myriad troubles could befall one of those teens—or be caused by them. Things he needed to be insured against—just in case some relative suddenly turned up to cite a violation that had in actuality never occurred.

She saw Jackson in a whole new, far more complicated light. He wasn't just a simple cowboy or even just a laid-back, drop-dead-gorgeous rancher. He was all that plus a businessman.

"Do you ever feel like chucking it all and going back to just being a rancher?" she asked him, curious.

Jackson continued walking along the perimeter, tedious though it seemed.

He thought her question over.

"Sometimes," he admitted. "But then I watch a kid get turned around and suddenly it all seems worth it. And, if you want to be technical about it, I was never really a rancher. What I did was help my uncle on the ranch after he straightened me out, but I never had a place of my own to run, at least not one that didn't involve working with hostile young guys who felt they'd been dealt a bum hand." He thought about his initial answer to her. "Seeing one of those get turned around, well, there's really nothing like it," he reiterated with feeling.

He'd been guiding Annabelle around the corral, keeping very close to the edges of the corral's perimeter as he talked with Debi and answered her questions. Before he knew it, he realized that he had come full circle and they were back at the entrance to the stables where they had started.

Not that he minded spending time with her like this, but it *was* getting late. Besides, he had a feeling that there were more than a couple of pairs of eyes watching him and Ryan's sister. He didn't want the boys to have anything more to talk about than he assumed they already had.

"How about calling it a night?" he suggested to Debi. "I think Annabelle's tired."

She had no idea how he could tell, but she wasn't about to argue or question his judgment. He had indulged her and she really appreciated it. "Whatever you say, Jackson," she answered.

Whatever he said. Jackson had to admit that he liked the sound of that.

The problem was, there were a lot of things he felt like saying to her.

A lot of things he felt like *doing* with her, as well. Neither of these impulses, he knew, was safe to act on. Not when he thought of the direction that either could take him or, for that matter, the consequences that lay at the end of either line.

Bringing Annabelle and her passenger back into the stable, he stopped just short of putting the horse into the stall.

Debi looked down at him. "Something wrong? Why did you stop?"

"Nothing's wrong," he told her, letting the end of the mare's reins touch the ground. The horse knew enough to remain where she was, as steadfast as if the reins had been tightly tied to a post, physically tethering her. "But it might be easier all around if you dismounted now, before I put Annabelle into her stall and take her saddle off."

"Sure," Debi said, more than happy to comply. But then she glanced down to the ground. Gauging the distance from where she was sitting to where she was supposed to step, she hesitated. It killed her to ask, but it was either that, or risk falling flat on her face in front of him.

Literally.

"Um, I think I might need a little help getting down," she said in a small voice.

Annabelle remained standing perfectly still. At least the horse was being cooperative, Jackson thought. Mov ing closer to the center of the mare, he raised his hands up toward Debi.

"Lean forward," he told her. When she did, he slipped his hands around her waist.

Debi sucked in a breath without meaning to. Her heart did a little dance within her chest, creating havoc.

No, she amended, *Jackson* was creating the havoc. She sincerely doubted that she would be reacting this way if she was being helped off her mount by someone who looked like an ogre out of a Grimm's fairy tale.

The next second, as she leaned down and put her hands on his shoulders for leverage, she felt Jackson's strong, capable hands gently tighten about her waist just before he eased her down.

That was when her body all but slid against his in one continuous motion.

She was only vaguely aware of her feet touching the ground. She was far more acutely aware of the fact that her body had made contact with his.

Soft against hard.

Warm waves went shooting not just up and down her spine but pretty much along the rest of her, as well. Her hands left his shoulders, but rather than falling to her sides, the way she had intended, they went in the other direction and somehow wound up going around the back of his neck.

Their eyes met and held. It seemed to her like things were being said without a single word being uttered.

Her breath caught in her throat. At the very least, she should be pushing him away—not pulling him in closer. This wasn't her. This wasn't the way that she normally behaved.

But nothing about this moment in the moonlight resembled her normal existence.

Debi had no idea who initiated the next move. Whether she was the one who tilted her head back, inviting his mouth to visit hers again, or if he made the first move, lowering his head—and his mouth—to hers.

She *shouldn't* be doing this, *couldn't* be allowing herself to get involved with a man, even *this* man. Her judgment was beyond poor. She couldn't risk using it and making another awful mistake.

The way she had with John.

Once a fool was *more* than enough, she knew that. And yet, somehow, she couldn't find it in herself to even *attempt* to resist.

She was drawn to this man who had done such miraculous things with teens—with Ryan—who everyone, including the system, had given up on.

Including?

Especially, she silently emphasized. Especially the system.

And even, secretly, her. She'd been precariously close, fractions of an inch away, to giving up on her brother.

Jackson had saved her from that. From the *despair* of that.

Jackson was at once her Lancelot, riding to the rescue, her miracle worker, and quite possibly the most compellingly sexy man she had ever met.

Debi melted into him, surrendering to the moment, to the kiss and to the man.

DAMN IT, HE KNEW this was wrong, knew he had no business being out here with her like this.

No business *doing* this.

She was technically a client, the guardian of one of his charges, for God's sake, and he was jeopardizing his standing by dropping his guard and going with his demanding needs.

What the hell was he *thinking*?

The sad truth of the matter was, he wasn't thinking. Not for one second. But oh, was he feeling. After being dead inside for so long, he was *feeling*.

He kissed the woman in his arms over and over again, living inside of the moment before the moment was somehow cruelly snatched away or just mysteriously disappeared into thin air.

But perversely, rather than satiate him, each kiss just made him that much hungrier for more.

Made him want *her* more.

Pulling Debi so close to him that they were in danger of fusing into one being, for one short moment, he allowed his imagination to go to places he'd never allowed it to venture before.

But then the common sense that had taken Sam so long to drill into his head reluctantly—but stubbornly—rose to reclaim its hold on him. They were inside the stable, but for all intents and purposes, they were still out in the open, still exposed.

He couldn't allow that to happen. She would suffer for it and he, he could lose at least some of the respect he had worked hard to build up.

She was worth it, a small voice whispered in his head.

Even so, he couldn't sacrifice the boys to his need for gratification.

Forcing himself to step back, he broke contact with Debi.

He said nothing. Protests filled his mind, scrambling

over one another, blotting out beginnings, blocking end-ings. He took a deep breath to try to regain control of himself.

"Good first lesson," Debi mumbled to him. "But I need to get back to the house. I'm very tired now and I should get an early start in the morning."

She was hoping he wouldn't ask her why because the second the words were out of her mouth, they sounded lame to her. Lame because she was making up the ex-cuse. She shouldn't have allowed herself to surrender to this, to something that she knew had no future, that barely had a life expectancy.

Certainly not beyond a week.

"I'll walk you," Jackson offered.

"No," she said a bit too quickly. "You take care of the horse. I'll be fine. It's not like the house is in the next county."

She was already crossing the stable's threshold, mov-ing outside as she said it.

Chapter Fifteen

She couldn't sleep.

It wasn't because of the heat. Granted, the day had been almost uncomfortably hot, but the heat had long since abated. The temperature in the world outside her open window had dropped by some fifteen degrees in the past few hours and there was even a rather sweet breeze coming in through the bedroom window.

Or, at least it wasn't because of the heat that existed *outside* of her. The heat inside of her was an entirely different story.

That heat had its roots in what had happened that evening in the stables, and rather than fading away after she had hurried back into the house, it clung to her.

Clung to her and blossomed.

Tired of tossing and turning, she got up and crossed to the window, hoping that if she stood there, eventually the breeze would cool her off.

It was a good theory. In execution, however, it fell flat—and almost painfully—on its figurative face.

This was absurd, Debi thought, disgusted with herself as she moved away from the window. She felt wide-awake and insanely restless. There was no way she was going to fall asleep like this.

How was she going to go to the clinic in the morning? She needed to be alert when she went to work. She owed as much to the doctors at the clinic, not to mention to the patients that came in.

But she wasn't exactly going to be fresh as a daisy by morning if she spent the night wide-awake because she was too wired to fall asleep.

By tomorrow morning, Debi thought in despair, she would be a zombie, not exactly someone thought to be an asset when it came to the medical field.

Pacing back and forth around the room and her rumpled bed, Debi dragged a hand through her tousled hair, frustrated and completely at a loss as to how to wind down.

But there was nothing she could do about it. Nothing that would help her resolve her situation or where her head was at...

Unless...

She stopped pacing and looked at the wall to her left. The wall that separated Jackson's bedroom from the one she was in.

Unless she retraced her dilemma back to its source.

Debi stared at the wall, thinking.

Maybe if she just talked to Jackson, she could also wind up talking herself down out of this strange, disconcerting place where her equally agitated mind and soul were currently residing, giving her no peace.

Summoning her courage—something that took her a bit of doing—she slipped on her robe, essentially a light, short scrap of blue that matched her equally short, equally blue nightgown.

She left her room, glancing up and down the hall to

make sure no one was around to witness this, then stood, waffling, in front of Jackson's door.

Twice she raised her right hand, her knuckles poised to knock, and twice she dropped her hand to her side, never having made contact with the door.

This is insane, she told herself in disgust. *Go lie down. Maybe you'll bore yourself to death and fall asleep that way.*

Turning on her bare heel, Debi started to go back to her room.

"Debi? Is something wrong?"

The sound of the deep voice behind her caused her heart to leap into her throat before she even turned back around to look at the man she was trying so hard to get out of her system.

He was bare-chested, the all but worn-out jeans he had on hanging seductively low on his taut hips. Breathing became a conscious effort for her. And having her heart lodged in her throat like this temporarily got in the way of her answering.

"I heard you pacing," Jackson told her when she said nothing. "Is something wrong?" he repeated.

Clearing her throat, Debi responded in a shaky voice, "Yes—and no."

"Multiple choice?" Jackson asked.

Her heart was back in place and pounding. Her fingertips felt almost damp and they were tingling.

She'd been a *married* woman for heaven's sakes. What was the matter with her? Why was she behaving like some adolescent girl facing her first teenage crush?

Because, for one thing, the man in front of her had a chest that seemed carved out of stone, and just looking at him made her pulse accelerate.

Taking a breath and trying to steady her capricious nerves, she moved closer to Jackson in order to speak quietly. "Listen, about what happened earlier…"

"I know," he told her, wanting to spare Debi the discomfort of talking about it. "You don't know what you were thinking," he said, taking a guess at what her excuse for kissing him with such intensity would be.

When he put it like that, when he handed her a readily crafted excuse for what she'd allowed to happen between them, it seemed to suddenly strip her of her indecisiveness and make the path before her almost crystal clear.

"Actually," she said softly, stepping into his room and then closing the door behind her without bothering to turn around or even spare it a single glance. "I do," she assured him softly. "I knew exactly what I was thinking then.

"Exactly what I'm thinking now," she added, her eyes on his. Suddenly, she felt as if she had been created with just this moment in mind.

The robe slipped from her shoulders, drifting to the floor and pooling there like a sigh.

Watching, mesmerized, he held back a ragged sigh.

How he wanted her.

And yet…

And yet he couldn't do this, couldn't allow this to happen. Not for the reasons he suspected lay at the very core of this for her.

Jackson framed her face with his hands, wanting her beyond belief, struggling to keep himself from acting on that feeling while blocking all those finely honed instincts that always rose to the forefront. The instincts that were so deeply entrenched in protecting lost souls and saving them.

Lost souls came in all sizes and shapes.

Some, he thought, belonged to big sisters who worried about their younger brothers caught in endless cycles of delinquent behavior.

The desire to protect this woman was tremendous. He realized that he needed to protect Debi from doing the wrong thing.

Needed, in this case, to protect her from himself.

Talk about being consigned to hell…

"I don't want this happening because you're feeling misplaced gratitude because of Ryan," he told her. That would be tantamount to his almost *preying* on her.

Debi placed a finger to his lips to keep Jackson from saying anything further.

"You saved Ryan and I'd have to be a robot not to feel something for you because of that," she whispered. "But it's not *just* that." She tilted her head back, bringing her mouth temptingly closer to his. "It's more. So much more."

What she was experiencing wasn't misplaced gratitude. Yes, it had sprung into being because of gratitude, but it was so much more than that.

What she felt for him intensified because he was trying to dissuade her. The man was incredibly selfless.

Her heart swelled.

"You're lonely," he guessed. Loneliness caused people to do foolish things they lived to regret. "Your jackass of a husband made you choose between him and Ryan— and when you did, he was outraged and insulted, so he left." Jackson searched her eyes for more insight as he spoke. "He didn't try to compromise or to negotiate, he just left. That had to hurt."

He wasn't given to violence, but he would have throttled the man for having hurt Debi this way.

Especially when he saw the tears,

She blinked back the tears that were now laced through her eyelashes. He had gotten it almost all right. "I'd forgotten. You know everything about what happened, don't you?"

"You did tell me some of it," he reminded her. "I looked into the rest." He'd done it to make sure that there wasn't something she was keeping back, something she was ashamed of. To his relief, she hadn't been physically abused. "Sheriff Santiago's got a deputy that knows her way around computers and search engines," he confessed. "She's gotten to be practically a wizard at it." Jackson paused, struggling between doing what he felt was the right thing—and taking what she was so generously offering him. "I just don't want you waking up tomorrow morning with regrets."

"If I do have regrets, it won't be because I made love with you," she told him softly. "It'll be because I didn't."

All the words he should have said to talk her out of this frame of mind fled as if they had been caught in a windstorm and swept out to sea. The next thing he was aware of was wrapping his arms around Debi, then feeling the soft contours of her body as it pressed up against the hardened, unyielding ridges of his.

But he was feeling far more than that.

Feeling guilt because he was unable to pull back, unable to lead her back to her room.

Unable to save her from herself—and from him, heaven help him.

But her mouth was so sweet, her body beyond tempting—and he was just a man.

A man with desires and weaknesses. A man who had gone through life, changed himself more than once, and when he'd finally got it right, had been so strict and demanding of himself that there had been—and was—no room for anything but the purpose, the calling that he had chosen: saving young lives by turning them around.

Companionship, romance and love, that was all for other people, people who didn't have something to atone for the way that he did. Who didn't have a debt to repay the way he did.

But this woman that fate—and her wayward brother—had brought to him, she made him forget all the rules that had been set in stone, all his silent promises to himself—and to the late uncle he would forever be grateful and indebted to.

This woman was, he felt quite simply, the fever in his blood—and his pending downfall as sure as day followed night.

Just kissing Debi gave him a rush, made his head spin.

Her nightgown—the bright blue scrap on her body—quickly became an afterthought as it found its way to the floor.

Jackson memorized her body with his hands before he ever actually laid his eyes on it. When he did, when he actually *looked* at her, he froze for a moment, stunned by how truly beautiful she was to him.

She had the body of goddess.

And a mouth that was made for sin, he thought the next moment.

His frayed, all but paper-thin jeans disappeared moments later. His body was totally primed for the final conquest, but he wanted her to derive as much pleasure from this as he could possibly give her. That meant placing more foreplay ahead of his own gratification.

Accustomed to all forms of self-denial, Jackson held

himself in check for as long as he could, making love to each part of her as if it was a separate entity as well as part of a greater, completely enticing whole.

He kissed her eyelids, the hollow of her throat, the nape of her neck before eventually working his way downward.

Using the tip of his tongue, he caressed her breasts, hardening the tips, finding a thrill in the way she moaned and shuddered in response before he worked his way to her belly, making it quiver.

And then, as the path took him ever lower, Jackson created a fire within her very core with teasing thrusts of his tongue.

Her movements beneath him grew in ever-increasing intensity and urgency.

Debi bucked and arched, grabbing fistfuls of the quilted cover beneath her on his bed. She all but bit through her lower lip to keep from crying out in sheer ecstasy as peak after peak rippled through her body that was so damp with sweat.

No one felt like this and lived, she thought, falling back against the bed, exhausted, after yet another climax had seized her and then burst apart like so many fireworks. She had no idea exactly what she had been doing those years she'd been married to John and they had purportedly been making love. But whatever it was, it didn't hold the *hint* of a candle to this.

This was what dying and going to heaven was all about, she couldn't help thinking.

And it wasn't over. Because the next moment, Jackson was there, his handsome, rugged face looming over hers, a soft, gentle look in his sensually seductive eyes

A very strange sensation darted into her. And stayed.

She reached up, placing her hands on either side of the hard planes and angles of his face. The next moment, she craned her neck so that she could reach his lips and press a kiss to them.

His arms closed around her, gathering her to him as he kissed her over and over again until she was more than ready—

Until she couldn't hold back anymore.

The next moment, he entered her, carefully, as if trying not to hurt her while giving in to what felt like an overwhelming need to possess her, to be one with her.

This was her other half.

This was how it was meant to be.

One whole from two halves.

Moving with urgency, Jackson increased his tempo by degrees, going faster and faster as she met him, movement for movement. Absorbing his rhythm.

They raced to the summit of the highest peak that stretched out before them. Raced until they came to the very top and then, still joined, still together, they experienced the inevitable mind-blowing explosion that embraced them in a cloud of ecstasy.

Pulses pounded like thunder as euphoria rained down on both of them. And when euphoria receded, he held on to her instead of the ebbing sensation, listening to the way her breathing slowed and became regular. Listening to her heart do the same.

But the feeling of well-being that had been created remained.

He smiled as his arms tightened around her. Jackson leaned over just slightly, kissing the top of her head, a deep affection spilling through him.

Tomorrow would come, as it always did, with its own set of problems, its own set of challenges. Very possibly, with its own set of regrets—hers, not his—no matter what she'd said. But tonight, tonight the warm glow of making love to a woman, of *loving* a woman for what he knew was the first time in his life, wove through his body, making him feel that everything else was secondary. That any obstacles would work themselves out because, after all, he had made love with what had turned out to be the perfect woman as well as his soul mate.

He had touched heaven.

"You okay?" he asked Debi. She'd been so quiet, he thought that she'd fallen asleep.

But she hadn't.

Debi smiled then, feeling far happier than she could remember being in a very long, long time. She turned her body into his.

"I'm perfect," she answered with a contented smile, all but intoxicated, tipsy on the giddiness still churning through her veins.

"Yes," Jackson agreed, wrapping his arm around her and drawing her closer still, "you are."

Chapter Sixteen

Jackson deliberately took the long way around the ranch house to avoid being seen. He made his way into the stables. He knew he'd be alone here this time of day and he really had to be alone to work out the tension and conflicting feelings that were even now doing battle inside of him.

One of the saddles needed mending and he put his mind to that.

Except that his mind was elsewhere and wasn't cooperating. A lot had happened in such a very short amount of time. Life-changing things. And it was all going to stop by tonight.

He stared at the saddle, not seeing it. Seeing something else entirely.

It had been a good run while it lasted, as Sam had been fond of saying toward the end.

Jackson pressed his lips together, saddened beyond words.

He'd had no examples to fall back on or to guide him when it came to male/female relationships. He never saw or heard anything but hot, angry words and cold silences exchanged between his own mother and father. No loving glances, no forgiving moments. None for each other and certainly none for him.

And both had left him, first his mother, eventually his father, neither one stopping to spare so much as a second glance in his direction or a word in parting. A byproduct of their marriage, he hadn't mattered to them just as their marriage hadn't mattered to them.

His father had cheated on his first wife with his second wife—the woman who had become his stepmother. And then he had cheated on her. And while his stepmother had done what she could to create a loving home for him and for his brother, that wasn't the same thing as being in a home with parents who loved and respected each other at its core.

While he had no example to guide him, he knew that Debi had a relationship that had failed her even though she had invested all of herself into it. She hadn't been able to see what was right in front of her and somehow wound up living a lie for more than a few years.

And yet, somehow, with all that holding them back, Debi and Jackson still seemed to trust one another, still reveled in what they had accidentally stumbled across and enjoyed.

Hesitantly, cautiously, they'd approached one another the morning after their first encounter with barely contained hope in their hearts. Hope that was quickly rewarded by the first word, the first smile. The first caress.

The first encounter turned out not to be an isolated one. Its existence bred another. And another. The night, Jackson felt, was their friend. And the calendar turned out to be their enemy because each day that went by brought him closer to the end.

The one he was facing now, he thought, his hands tightening on the fraying saddle cinch he was supposed to be repairing.

The boys who were brought to him had an average time in which their behavior would come around, if that was actually in their cards—and so far it always had been.

Some took more time, some took less, but a reversal in behavior usually occurred somewhere around a total of four weeks.

Ryan took less time to begin to come around. It was longer than two, but slightly less than three. Slightly less than three weeks to see that there was not just hope, but a definite reversal of behavior in the offing.

So Jackson braced himself. He knew in his heart that Debi would be leaving soon. Leaving because he had restored her brother to his former self.

Leaving because he had a knack for what he did, was good at it, so there was no longer an excuse for her to stay.

It was in his power to prolong the process, to drag it out and say things that would create stumbling blocks to reaching the desired final goal. But that would be unfair and selfish and he had learned not to be that way because years ago a good man had made him change his ways and his outlook.

Stretched, Ryan's complete return to decent behavior took a little more than four weeks. Jackson couldn't honestly pretend he needed any longer than that.

And now his honesty was going to cause him to lose the only complete happiness he'd ever known.

Jackson bit off the curse that rose in his throat then tried to focus in on his work.

He failed.

"You look like you've just lost your best friend." Garrett commented.

"What?" Preoccupied, Jackson stared at his younger

brother uncomprehendingly. It took a couple of moments to replay Garrett's words so that they registered in his head. "Oh, no, not yet anyway."

"But you're going to?" Garrett questioned, then rephrased his question. "You're going to lose your best friend? Hey, I didn't know I was going anywhere," he kidded.

Jackson didn't smile.

"You want to talk about it?" Garrett gently prodded, drawing closer.

Jackson avoided making eye contact. "No."

"Worse than I thought," Garrett said, leaning against the stall right next to his brother and giving the impression that he wasn't about to go anywhere. "Look, don't play the noble, stoic Navajo warrior with me, you're only half Native American. The other half of you is Caucasian. That's the talkative half," Garrett instructed. "What's bothering you?"

This time Jackson *did* look at his brother. "Other than you?"

"Yeah, other than me."

Jackson turned his face away from him and looked back to the saddle repairs he had barely made a dent in. "I don't want to talk about it."

Garrett shrugged. "You want to play hard to get? That's fine by me." He shifted so that he was in front of Jackson and his brother was forced to look at him. "I've got all day."

Jackson took a step, only to have his brother emulate it, matching him move for move. "You're just going to stand there, blocking my way?"

Garrett's laid-back grin seemed to spread from ear to ear. "Yup."

Jackson drew himself up. He was taller, although Garrett was the more muscular one. "What makes you think I'll let you? That I won't just pick you up and toss you out of my way?" Jackson challenged.

Garrett shrugged nonchalantly, unfazed. "Because you're not a bully anymore. Because that's not who you ever really were, at bottom. So spill it," he ordered in a relatively quiet voice. "What's got you all pensive and sullen like this?" Garrett asked.

Jackson debated pushing his brother aside and storming away, but Garrett was right. This wasn't him. And while he had never been one to consciously spill out his insides—or want to—he knew Garrett. His younger brother was nothing if not persistent. He would keep after him until he got the answers he was looking for.

There was nothing to be gained by holding out on him. So he didn't.

"She's leaving."

"You saw her packing," he concluded, his tone compassionate.

Jackson's was both resigned and frustrated. "Yeah."

"Have you talked to her?"

There was a long, exasperated pause before Jackson finally replied, "No."

Garrett stared at his older brother as if Jackson had just grown another head.

"No?" he questioned in disbelief. "You didn't talk to her?"

"I said no," Jackson snapped, irritated.

"Let me get this straight. You obviously care about the woman—and from what I and the immediate world can see, the feeling is mutual—and you *haven't talked to her about staying?*" he demanded, his voice rising an octave, possibly two.

"What part of 'no' don't you understand?" Jackson shouted back.

"All of it," Garrett retorted. "Go, talk to her," he ordered Jackson. "Tell the woman you don't want her to leave."

But Jackson stubbornly remained exactly where he was. He was *not* about to beg—especially not when he felt it wouldn't do any good.

"If she didn't want to leave, she wouldn't," Jackson maintained.

Garrett could only shake his head in completely frustrated wonder. "Women are right, some men can be so dumb."

Jackson's eyes narrowed as he glared at his younger brother. "Are you calling me dumb?"

"Yes, I am," he shot back, going toe-to-toe with Jackson. "Did it ever occur to you that she's leaving because you haven't asked her to stay? That she feels that as far as you're concerned, this was just a nice little interlude, but now it's over and it's time for her to go back home the way you always knew she had to?"

"She doesn't think that," Jackson protested angrily.

"How do you know?" Garrett challenged. "You never talked to her about this."

A malevolent look washed over Jackson's features, then gave way to the realization that his brother was right. "You're annoying," he told Garrett.

The corners of Garrett's generous mouth curved. "You're only saying that because you know I'm right."

Jackson opened his mouth, then shut it again. Exasperation all but seeped out of every pore as he glared at his younger brother. Glared at him until Jackson abruptly turned on the heel of his boot and stormed out of the stable.

He had somewhere else to be.

"Remember to use your words, Jackson," Garrett called after him. "The woman's not a mind reader."

Jackson made no parting comment. He was too busy framing what he was going to say to Debi. He had to get this right.

Because he felt as if his very life depended on it.

DAMN HIM, ANYWAY.

Jackson knew she was leaving today and he hadn't said anything about it.

Not one single word.

Last night, he'd come to her bedroom, the way he had every other night since they'd first been together, and they'd made love. Wonderful, glorious love, the way they always did.

But afterward, when they lay there and he'd held her in his arms, Jackson didn't say anything. Didn't talk about what they both knew was happening today. Didn't even comment on Ryan and his complete about-face from being the angry, troubled teen who'd first crossed The Healing Ranch's threshold.

Nothing.

Not one single word.

He'd acted just like the next day— *this* day—was just another day instead of her last one here with him. Hers and Ryan's.

What that told her was that she had an unblemished track record, she thought bitterly. She *still* couldn't pick

'em. Couldn't pick a man to care about who would ultimately care about her.

Pick a man? Debi thought, mocking herself. Damn it,
she didn't just "pick" him, she fell in *love* with him. In
love with a man who didn't even care enough to come
to see her today.

She stared down at the suitcase she'd finished packing more than an hour ago and blinked. A teardrop fell,
landing on her tank top. It darkened the strawberry color
as the moisture sank into the material.

"Stupid, stupid, stupid," she admonished herself, angrily wiping away the wet stain left on her cheek. Why
was she crying? He wasn't worth it. The entire male spe-
cies wasn't worth it.

Except for Ryan, she reminded herself. She had to
think of her brother, not herself, she silently lectured. She
had to remember that leaving here was going to be hard
for him, too. He'd made friends here, worthwhile friends.
Friends she knew he was going to remain in contact with.

Unlike Jackson with her.

The sigh shuddered through her as she let the suitcase
lid fall into place. She snapped the locks closed one at
a time. She had to stop stalling, Debi upbraided herself.
The drive back to Indianapolis was a long one.

She was already tired.

Dragging the suitcase off the bed, she deposited it on
the floor just as she heard the light knock on her door.

Ryan, she thought.

He'd finally found his manners. She could thank Jackson for that, too.

Debi pressed her lips together, struggling to bank
down the emotions that threatened to burst through. She

told herself not to think of Jackson. Not now. She wasn't strong enough to deal with that now.

The knock came again, more forcefully this time.

"It's open," she called to her brother. "I'm almost read—"

She didn't finish the word because she forgot it. Forgot everything.

Everything but the man standing in the doorway.

"Jackson."

He had no memory of crossing the threshold, or of entering the room. The sound of her voice just pulled him in, blotting out everything else but her, and his overwhelming need for her.

All the carefully selected words he'd rehearsed in his head walking here completely vanished, leaving him with only two.

"Don't go." He took her hands in his, his eyes pleading with her. "I know I have no right to ask this. I know that your whole life is back in Indianapolis. But if you go, you'll take my whole life with you. Because you *are* my whole life and if you leave, I won't have a reason to breathe.

"I won't be *able* to breathe," he emphasized. He pressed the hands he was holding against his chest, to his heart, his eyes still not leaving hers. "Is there anything, *anything* I can say to get you to reconsider and stay?"

For a second, she didn't say anything. *Couldn't* say anything. She'd wanted this so much, had longed for it so hard, that now that it was actually happening, that she was actually *hearing* him say it, it didn't seem real and the ability to form words, let alone the right words, momentarily deserted her.

"I can't, can I?" Jackson said, guessing at the reason

for her silence. "I'm sorry," he whispered, misunderstanding.

"No, no," Debi cried, finally finding her voice. "You already said it," she told him. He eyed her quizzically and she explained, "You asked me not to go."

"Then you'll stay?" he asked, almost afraid to believe her even as he pulled her to him with one arm, sealing her to his chest.

The tears insisted on coming again, but this time she laughed through them.

"You just try to get rid of me," she dared.

"Maybe in a hundred years—or two," he speculated just before he brought his mouth down to hers—and pushed the door to her room closed with his free hand.

Epilogue

"I'm not, like, going to be Debi's maid of honor or any-thing like that, am I?" Ryan asked Garrett uncertainly as he tried to watch what he was doing.

The latter was helping him tie the black bow tie he was supposed to be wearing to his sister's wedding. Never having worn one before—hardly ever having even *seen* one before—he had no idea where to even begin.

"I mean, I love her and all. There's nobody I love more—and I really care about Jackson, too," he quickly assured the groom's young brother. "But a guy's gotta keep an eye out for his overall reputation, you know? People would always remember something like his being a maid of honor for his sister, even if he became some-thing important—like the owner of a baseball team, or something like that."

It was clear that the idea of being seen as acting less than manly really worried Ryan.

"You finished?" Garrett asked after patiently allow-ing the fifteen-year-old to vent and get all his questions as well as all his insecurities out of his system.

Ryan paused for a moment and thought. After reflect-ing, he quietly answered, "Yeah, I guess so."

"You 'guess so'?" Garrett repeated.

Ryan blew out a breath. He had to remember to think before he talked. Jackson had drilled that into him. "I'm finished," he confirmed quietly.

"Good, because you're *not* a maid of honor or a bridesmaid, or anything that remotely has to do with the word *maid*." Garrett paused to survey his efforts in the mirror that had been brought into the room for this exact purpose. With a nod, he accepted what he saw. "You're a co–best man."

"Does that mean that we're supposed to be joined together somehow, like those twins that need to be separated with operations 'cause they couldn't go anyplace without each other?"

Rather than acting surprised or taken aback at the question—or worse, laughing—Garrett just took it in stride. "No, in this case it means 'jointly,' like you and I have the same position in this wedding. Jackson wanted both of us to be his best man because he couldn't choose between us."

There was a little more to it than that, Garrett added silently. His brother wanted to make sure that he didn't hurt the teen's feelings, but he hadn't wanted to just sell out and leave *Garrett* in the cold, either. So this awkward setup was the solution—so far.

"Oh." Dressed, ready, the teen paused again, reviewing the situation—and his options, as well as his sister's. This was her second marriage and he wanted it to go right. "But Debi doesn't have anyone to walk alongside her—or to give her away," Ryan realized.

Garrett looked at the teen. This would be a perfect way to even things out. "Would you rather do that than be a co–best man?"

It was obvious from the expression on his face that he

would. "You think Jackson would be okay with that?" he asked, concerned.

Garrett smiled. It was amazing, the effect his older brother had on these boys.

"I think that Jackson would be just fine with that. Your sister comes first with him and I think she'd like you walking her down the aisle," he told Ryan.

Ryan bobbed his head up and down in agreement, then suddenly stopped. "I'm not really going to be giving her away, am I?" Ryan asked hesitantly. "I mean, she's still going to be my sister, right?"

"Until the end of time," Garrett poetically affirmed. He paused to straighten Ryan's bow tie again just a fraction of an inch. "You look great, kid," he said, patting the teen on the shoulder. "I'm just going to go check on Jackson. Wedding's starting in about ten minutes," he told Ryan, glancing at his watch. "Look alive," was his parting comment.

Garrett made his way to his brother's downstairs office. Everything had been temporarily cleared away so that Jackson could use the office to get ready for his wedding. Debi told him that she didn't care what he wore, that she would marry him in his jeans and work shirt, but he had opted to make it formal for her.

Surprising them, Miss Joan had come through with tuxedos brought in from Dallas for Jackson, him and Ryan, as well. The tuxedos were rentals—Miss Joan knew someone who knew someone—but Debi's wedding gown, it turned out, was a gift.

"I never had a daughter to fuss over," Miss Joan told a stunned Debi when the latter began to protest that she couldn't allow the woman to do that. "This at least allows me to get a peek at what it might have been like.

You can't deny an old woman that." This statement had been her way of sealing the deal.

Debi couldn't argue with that.

"Hey, you look almost handsome," Garrett noted as he opened the door and looked in on his brother.

The truth of it was, he'd never seen Jackson look so regal. He would have even said "noble" if it hadn't struck him that it might sound stereotypical to say as much.

Jackson turned to face his brother. "Is it normal to feel like I'm about to throw up?" he asked. He wasn't supposed to be feeling sick, he was supposed to be feeling elated, he admonished himself.

"Very normal, I hear. You look good," Garrett told him.

"I feel like hell," Jackson confided.

"It'll pass," Garrett assured him.

"You're awfully insightful for a single guy," Jackson accused his brother.

"I know," Garrett replied, his face completely unexpressive. "By the way, you're down to one best man."

"How did you manage that?" Jackson asked, impressed.

"Debi needed someone to give her away."

Jackson smiled. He knew he could count on his brother to make things come around. "Good thinking."

"Actually, Ryan was the one to bring it up, but I might have been the one to set the stage," Garrett added with a conspiratorial smile.

The sound of twin guitars playing the opening strains of the "Wedding March" could be heard through the open windows, coming from the rear garden.

"Better hustle, Jackson," Garrett prodded. "It sounds like we're good to go."

Jackson pressed a hand to his abdomen as he walked out of the room. "I think I really am going to be sick."

Garrett took his elbow and steered his brother through the hall toward the gathering beneath a flowered trellis outside. "I guarantee you'll forget all about that the second you see Debi coming toward you in that wedding gown."

And he did.

* * * * *

Staten

WHEN HER OLD hall clock chimed eleven times, Staten
Kirkland left Quinn O'Grady's bed. While she slept, he
dressed in the shadows, watching her with only the light
of the full moon. She'd given him what he needed tonight, and, as always, he felt as if he'd given her nothing.

Walking out to her porch, he studied the newly washed
earth, thinking of how empty his life was except for these
few hours he shared with Quinn. He'd never love her or
anyone, but he wished he could do something for her.
Thanks to hard work and inherited land, he was a rich
man. She was making a go of her farm, but barely. He
could help her if she'd let him. But he knew she'd never
let him.

As he pulled on his boots, he thought of a dozen things
he could do around the place. Like fixing that old tractor out in the mud or modernizing her irrigation system.
The tractor had been sitting out by the road for months. If
she'd accept his help, it wouldn't take him an hour to pull
the old John Deere out and get the engine running again.

Only, she wouldn't accept anything from him. He
knew better than to ask.

He wasn't even sure they were friends some days.
Maybe they were more. Maybe less. He looked down at

his palm, remembering how she'd rubbed cream on it and worried that all they had in common was loss and the need, now and then, to touch another human being.

The screen door creaked. He turned as Quinn, wrapped in an old quilt, moved out into the night.

"I didn't mean to wake you," he said as she tiptoed across the snow-dusted porch. "I need to get back. Got eighty new yearlings coming in early." He never apologized for leaving, and he wasn't now. He was simply stating facts. With the cattle rustling going on and his plan to enlarge his herd, he might have to hire more men. As always, he felt as though he needed to be on his land and on alert.

She nodded and moved to stand in front of him.

Staten waited. They never touched after they made love. He usually left without a word, but tonight she obviously had something she wanted to say.

Another thing he probably did wrong, he thought. He never complimented her, never kissed her on the mouth, never said any words after he touched her. If she didn't make little sounds of pleasure now and then, he wouldn't have been sure he satisfied her.

Now, standing so close to her, he felt more a stranger than a lover. He knew the smell of her skin, but he had no idea what she was thinking most of the time. She knew quilting and how to make soap from her lavender. She played the piano like an angel and didn't even own a TV. He knew ranching and watched from his recliner every game the Dallas Cowboys played.

If they ever spent over an hour talking they'd probably figure out they had nothing in common. He'd played every sport in high school, and she'd played in both the orchestra and the band. He'd collected most of his college hours online, and she'd gone all the way to New York to school. But they'd loved the same person Amalah had been Quinn's best friend and his one love. Only, they rarely talked about how they felt. Not anymore. Not ever, really. It was too painful, he guessed, for both of them.

Tonight the air was so still, moisture hung like invisible lace. She looked to be closer to her twenties than her forties. Quinn had her own quiet kind of beauty. She always had, and he guessed she still would even when she was old.

To his surprise, she leaned in and kissed his mouth.

He watched her. "You want more?" he finally asked, figuring it was probably the dumbest thing to say to a naked woman standing two inches away from him. He had no idea what *more* would be. They always had sex once, if they had it at all, when he knocked on her door. Sometimes neither made the first move, and they just cuddled on the couch and held each other. Quinn wasn't a passionate woman. What they did was just satisfying a need that they both had now and then.

She kissed him again without saying a word. When her cheek brushed against his stubbled chin, it was wet and tasted newborn like the rain.

Slowly, Staten moved his hands under her blanket and circled her warm body, then he pulled her closer and kissed her fully like he hadn't kissed a woman since his wife died.

Her lips were soft and inviting. When he opened her mouth and invaded, it felt far more intimate than anything they had ever done, but he didn't stop. She wanted this from him, and he had no intention of denying her. No one would ever know that she was the thread that kept him together some days.

When he finally broke the kiss, Quinn was out of breath. She pressed her forehead against his jaw and he waited.

"From now on," she whispered so low he felt her words more than heard them, "when you come to see me, I need you to kiss me goodbye before you go. If I'm asleep, wake me. You don't have to say a word, but you have to kiss me."

She'd never asked him for anything. He had no intention of saying no. His hand spread across the small of her back and pulled her hard against him. "I won't forget if that's what you want." He could feel her heart pounding and knew her asking had not come easy.

She nodded. "It's what I want."

He brushed his lips over hers, loving the way she sighed as if wanting more before she pulled away.

"Good night," she said as though rationing pleasure. Stepping inside, she closed the screen door between them.

Raking his hair back, he put on his hat as he watched her fade into the shadows. The need to return was already building in him. "I'll be back Friday night if it's all right. It'll be late, I've got to visit with my grandmother and do her list of chores before I'll be free. If you like, I could bring barbecue for supper?" He felt as if he was rambling, but something needed to be said, and he had no idea what.

"And vegetables," she suggested.

He nodded. She wanted a meal, not just the meat. "I'll have them toss in sweet potato fries and okra."

She held the blanket tight as if he might see her body. She didn't meet his eyes when he added, "I enjoyed kissing you, Quinn. I look forward to doing so again."

With her head down, she nodded as she vanished into the darkness without a word.

He walked off the porch, deciding if he lived to be a hundred he'd never understand Quinn. As far as he knew, she'd never had a boyfriend when they were in school. And his wife had never told him about Quinn dating anyone special when she went to New York to that fancy music school. Now, in her forties, she'd never had a date, much less a lover that he knew of. But she hadn't been a virgin when they'd made love the first time.

Asking her about her love life seemed far too personal a question.

Climbing into his truck, he forced his thoughts toward problems at the ranch. He needed to hire men; they'd lost three cattle to rustlers this month. As he planned the coming day, Staten did what he always did: he pushed Quinn to a corner of his mind, where she'd wait until he saw her again.

As he passed through the little town of Crossroads, all the businesses were closed up tight except for a gas station that stayed open twenty-four hours to handle the few travelers needing to refuel or brave enough to sample their food.

Half a block away from the station was his grandmother's bungalow, dark amid the cluster of senior citizens' homes. One huge light in the middle of all the little homes shone a low glow onto the porch of each house. The tiny white cottages reminded him of a circle of wagons camped just off the main road. She'd lived fifty years on Kirkland land, but when Staten's granddad, her husband, had died, she'd wanted to move to town. She'd been a teacher in her early years and said she needed to be with her friends in the retirement community, not alone in the big house on the ranch.

He swore without anger, remembering all her instructions the day she moved to town. She wanted her only grandson to drop by every week to switch out batteries, screw in lightbulbs and reprogram the TV that she'd spent the week messing up. He didn't mind dropping by. Besides his father, who considered his home—when he wasn't in Washington—to be Dallas, Granny was the only family Staten had.

A quarter mile past the one main street of Crossroads, his truck lights flashed across four teenagers walking along the road between the Catholic church and the gas station.

Three boys and a girl. Fifteen or sixteen, Staten guessed.

For a moment the memory of Randall came to mind. He'd been about their age when he'd crashed, and he'd worn the same type of blue-and-white letter jacket that two of the boys wore tonight.

Staten slowed as he passed them. "You kids need a ride?" The lights were still on at the church, and a few cars were in the parking lot. Saturday night, Staten remembered. Members of 4-H would probably be working in the basement on projects.

One kid waved. A tall Hispanic boy named Lucas, whom he thought was the oldest son of the head wrangler on the Collins Ranch. Reyes was his last name, and Staten remembered the boy being one of a dozen young kids who were often hired part-time at the ranch.

Staten had heard the kid was almost as good a wrangler as his father. The magic of working with horses must have been passed down from father to son, along with the height. Young Reyes might be lean but, thanks to working, he would be in better shape than either of the football boys. When Lucas Reyes finished high school, he'd have no trouble hiring on at any of the big ranches, including the Double K.

"No, we're fine, Mr. Kirkland," the Reyes boy said politely. "We're just walking down to the station for a Coke. Reid Collins's brother is picking us up soon."

"No crime in that, mister," a redheaded kid in a letter jacket answered. His words came fast and clipped, reminding Staten of how his son had sounded.

Volume from a boy trying to prove he was a man, Staten thought.

He couldn't see the faces of the two boys with letter jackets, but the girl kept her head up. "We've been working on a project for the fair," she answered politely. "I'm Lauren Brigman, Mr. Kirkland."

Staten nodded *Sheriff Brigman's daughter, I remember you*. She knew enough to be polite, but it was none of his business. "Good evening, Lauren," he said. "Nice to see you again. Good luck with the project."

When he pulled away, he shook his head. Normally, he wouldn't have bothered to stop. This might be small-town Texas, but they were not his problem. If he saw the Reyes boy again, he would apologize.

Staten swore. At this rate he'd turn into a nosy old man by forty-five. It didn't seem that long ago that he and Amalah used to walk up to the gas station after meetings at the church.

Hell, maybe Quinn asking to kiss him had rattled him more than he thought. He needed to get his head straight. She was just a friend. A woman he turned to when the storms came. Nothing more. That was the way they both wanted it.

Until he made it back to her porch next Friday night, he had a truckload of trouble at the ranch to worry about.

Lauren

A MIDNIGHT MOON blinked its way between storm clouds as Lauren Brigman cleaned the mud off her shoes. The guys had gone inside the gas station for Cokes. She didn't really want anything to drink, but it was either walk over with the others after working on their fair projects or stay back at the church and talk to Mrs. Patterson.

Somewhere Mrs. Patterson had gotten the idea that since Lauren didn't have a mother around, she should take every opportunity to have a "girl talk" with the sheriff's daughter.

Lauren wanted to tell the old woman that she had known all the facts of life by the age of seven, and she really did not need a buddy to share her teenage years with. Besides, her mother lived in Dallas. It wasn't like she'd died. She'd just left. Just because she couldn't stand the sight of Lauren's dad didn't mean she didn't call and talk to Lauren almost every week. Maybe Mom had just gotten tired of the sheriff's nightly lectures. Lauren had heard every one of Pop's talks so many times that she had them memorized in alphabetical order.

Her grades put her at the top of the sophomore class, and she saw herself bound for college in less than three years. Lauren had no intention of getting pregnant, or doing drugs, or any of the other fearful situations Mrs. Patterson and her father had hinted might befall her. Her pop didn't even want her dating until she was sixteen, and, judging from the boys she knew in high school, she'd just as soon go dateless until eighteen. Maybe college would have better pickings. Some of these guys were so dumb she was surprised they got their cowboy hats on straight every morning.

Reid Collins walked out from the gas station first with a can of Coke in each hand. "I bought you one even though you said you didn't want anything to drink," he announced as he neared. "Want to lean on me while you clean your shoes?"

Lauren rolled her eyes. Since he'd grown a few inches and started working out, Reid thought he was God's gift to girls.

"Why?" she asked as she tossed the stick. "I have a brick wall to lean on. And don't get any ideas we're on a date, Reid, just because I walked over here with you."

"I don't date sophomores," he snapped. "I'm on first string, you know. I could probably date any senior I want to. Besides, you're like a little sister, Lauren. We've known each other since you were in the first grade."

She thought of mentioning that playing first string on a football team that only had forty players total, including the coaches and water boy, wasn't any great accomplishment, but arguing with Reid would rot her brain. He'd been born rich, and he'd thought he knew everything since he cleared the birth canal. She feared his disease was terminal.

"If you're cold, I'll let you wear my football jacket." When she didn't comment, he bragged, "I had to reorder a bigger size after a month of working out."

She hated to, but if she didn't compliment him soon, he'd never stop begging. "You look great in the jacket, Reid. Half the seniors on the team aren't as big as you." There was nothing wrong with Reid from the neck down. In a few years he'd be a knockout with the Collins good looks and trademark rusty hair, not quite brown, not quite red. But he still wouldn't interest her.

"So, when I get my driver's license next month, do you want to take a ride?"

Lauren laughed. "You've been asking that since I was in the third grade and you got your first bike. The answer is still no. We're friends, Reid. We'll always be friends, I'm guessing."

He smiled a smile that looked as if he'd been practicing. "I know, Lauren, but I keep wanting to give you a chance now and then. You know, some guys don't want to date the sheriff's daughter, and I hate to point it out, babe, but if you don't fill out some, it's going to be bad news in college." He had the nerve to point at her chest.

"I know." She managed to pull off a sad look. "Having my father is a cross I have to bear. Half the guys in town are afraid of him. Like he might arrest them for talking to me. Which he might." She had no intention of discussing her lack of curves with Reid.

"No, it's not fear of him, exactly," Reid corrected. "I think it's more the bullet holes they're afraid of. Every time a guy looks at you, your old man starts patting his service weapon. Nerve-racking habit, if you ask me. From the looks of it, I seem to be the only one he'll let stand beside you, and that's just because our dads are friends."

She grinned. Reid was spoiled and conceited and self-centered, but he was right. They'd probably always be friends. Her dad was the sheriff, and his was the mayor of Crossroads, even though he lived five miles from town on one of the first ranches established near Ransom Canyon.

With her luck, Reid would be the only guy in the state that her father would let her date. Grumpy old Pop had what she called Terminal Cop Disease. Her father thought everyone, except his few friends, was most likely a criminal, anyone under thirty should be stopped and searched, and anyone who'd ever smoked pot could not be trusted.

Tim O'Grady, Reid's eternal shadow, walked out of the station with a huge frozen drink. The clear cup showed off its red-and-yellow layers of cherry-and-pineapple-flavored sugar.

Where Reid was balanced in his build, Tim was lanky, disjointed. He seemed to be made of mismatched parts. His arms were too long. His feet seemed too big, and his wired smile barely fit in his mouth. When he took a deep draw on his drink, he staggered and held his forehead from the brain freeze.

Lauren laughed as he danced around like a puppet with his strings crossed. Timothy, as the teachers called him, was always good for a laugh. He had the depth of cheap paint but the imagination of a natural-born storyteller.

"Maybe I shouldn't have gotten an icy drink on such a cold night," he mumbled between gulps. "If I freeze from the inside out, put me up on Main Street as a statue."

Lauren giggled.

Lucas Reyes was the last of their small group to come outside. Lucas hadn't bought anything, but he evidently was avoiding standing outside with her. She'd known Lucas Reyes for a few years, maybe longer, but he never talked to her. Like Reid and Tim, he was a year ahead of her, but since he rarely talked, she usually only noticed him as a background person in her world.

Unlike them, Lucas didn't have a family name following him around opening doors for a hundred miles.

They all four lived east of Crossroads along the rambling canyon called Ransom Canyon. Lauren and her father lived in one of a cluster of houses near the lake, as did Tim's parents. Reid's family ranch was five miles farther out. She had no idea where Lucas's family lived. Maybe on the Collins Ranch. His father worked on the Bar W, which had been in the Collins family for over a hundred years. The area around the headquarters looked like a small village.

Reid repeated the plan. "My brother said he'd drop Sharon off and be back for us. But if they get busy doing their thing it could be an hour. We might as well walk back and sit on the church steps."

"Great fun," Tim complained. "Everything's closed. It's freezing out here, and I swear this town is so dead somebody should bury it."

"We could start walking toward home," Lauren suggested as she pulled a tiny flashlight from her key chain. The canyon lake wasn't more than a mile. If they walked they wouldn't be so cold. She could probably be home before Reid's dumb brother could get his lips off Sharon. If rumors were true, Sharon had very kissable lips, among other body parts.

"Better than standing around here," Reid said as Tim kicked mud toward the building. "I'd rather be walking than sitting. Plus, if we go back to the church, Mrs. Patterson will probably come out to keep us company."

Without a vote, they started walking. Lauren didn't like the idea of stumbling into mud holes now covered up by a dusting of snow along the side of the road, but it sounded better than standing out front of the gas station. Besides, the moon offered enough light, making the tiny flashlight her father insisted she carry worthless.

Within a few yards, Reid and Tim had fallen behind

and were lighting up a smoke. To her surprise, Lucas stayed beside her.

"You don't smoke?" she asked, not really expecting him to answer.

"No, can't afford the habit," he said, surprising her. "I've got plans, and they don't include lung cancer."

Maybe the dark night made it easier to talk, or maybe Lauren didn't want to feel so alone in the shadows. "I was starting to think you were a mute. We've had a few classes together, and you've never said a word. Even to-night you were the only one who didn't talk about your project."

Lucas shrugged. "Didn't see the point. I'm just enter-ing for the prize money, not trying to save the world or build a better tomorrow."

She giggled.

He laughed, too, realizing he'd just made fun of the whole point of the projects. "Plus," he added, "there's just not much opportunity to get a word in around those two." He nodded his head at the two letter jackets falling farther behind as a cloud of smoke haloed above them.

She saw his point. The pair trailed them by maybe twenty feet or more, and both were talking about foot-ball. Neither seemed to require a listener.

"Why do you hang out with them?" she asked. Lucas didn't seem to fit. Studious and quiet, he hadn't gone out for sports or joined many clubs that she knew about. "Jocks usually hang out together."

"I wanted to work on my project tonight, and Reid of-fered me a ride. Listening to football talk beats walking in this weather."

Lauren tripped into a pothole. Lucas's hand shot out

and caught her in the darkness. He steadied her, then let go.

"Thanks. You saved my life," she joked.

"Hardly, but if I had, you'd owe me a blood debt."

"Would I have to pay?"

"Of course. It would be a point of honor. You'd have to save me or be doomed to a coward's hell."

"Lucky you just kept me from tripping, or I'd be following you around for years waiting to repay the debt." She rubbed her arm where he'd touched her. He was stronger than she'd thought he would be. "You lift weights?"

The soft laughter came again. "Yeah, it's called work. Until I was sixteen, I spent the summers and every weekend working on Reid's father's ranch. Once I was old enough, I signed up at the Kirkland place to cowboy when they need extras. Every dime I make is going to college tuition in a year. That's why I don't have a car yet. When I get to college, I won't need it, and the money will go toward books."

"But you're just a junior. You've still got a year and a half of high school."

"I've got it worked out so I can graduate early. High school's a waste of time. I've got plans. I can make a hundred-fifty a day working, and my dad says he thinks I'll be able to cowboy every day I'm not in school this spring and all summer."

She tripped again, and his hand steadied her once more. Maybe it was her imagination, but she swore he held on a little longer than necessary.

"You're an interesting guy, Lucas Reyes."

"I will be," he said. "Once I'm in college, I can still come home and work breaks and weekends. I'm thinking I can take a few online classes during the summer, live at home and save enough to pay for the next year. I'm going to Tech no matter what it takes."

"You planning on getting through college in three years, too?"

He shook his head. "Don't know if I can. But I'll have the degree, whatever it is, before I'm twenty-two."

No one her age had ever talked of the future like that. Like they were just passing through this time in their life and something yet to come mattered far more. "When you are somebody, I think I'd like to be your friend."

"I hope we will be more than that, Lauren." His words were so low, she wasn't sure she heard them.

"Hey, you two deadbeats up there!" Reid yelled. "I got an idea."

Lauren didn't want the conversation with Lucas to end, but if she ignored Reid he'd just get louder. "What?"

Reid ran up between them and put an arm over both her and Lucas's shoulders. "How about we break into the Gypsy House? I hear it's haunted by gypsies who died a hundred years ago."

Tim caught up to them. As always, he agreed with Reid. "Look over there in the trees. The place is just waiting for us. Heard if you rattle a gypsy's bones, the dead will speak to you." Tim's eyes glowed in the moonlight. "I had a cousin once who said he heard voices in that old place, and no one was there but him."

"This is not a good idea." Lauren tried to back away, but Reid held her shoulder tight.

"Come on, Lauren, for once in your life, do something that's not safe. No one's lived in the old place for years. How much trouble can we get into?"

Tim's imagination had gone wild. According to him all kinds of things could happen. They might find a body.

Ghosts could run them out, or the spirit of a gypsy might take over their minds. Who knew, zombies might sleep in the rubble of old houses.

Lauren rolled her eyes. She didn't want to think of the zombies getting Tim. A walking dead with braces was too much.

"It's just a rotting old house," Lucas said so low no one heard but Lauren. "There's probably rats or rotten floors. It's an accident waiting to happen. How about you come back in the daylight, Reid, if you really want to explore the place?"

"We're all going, now," Reid announced, as he shoved Lauren off the road and into the trees that blocked the view of the old homestead from passing cars. "Think of the story we'll have to tell everyone Monday. We will have explored a haunted house and lived to tell the tale."

Reason told her to protest more strongly, but at fifteen, reason wasn't as intense as the possibility of an adventure. Just once, she'd have a story to tell. Just this once... her father wouldn't find out.

They rattled across the rotting porch steps fighting tumbleweeds that stood like flimsy guards around the place. The door was locked and boarded up. The smell of decay hung in the foggy air, and a tree branch scraped against one side of the house as if whispering for them to stay back.

The old place didn't look like much. It might have been the remains of an early settlement, built solid to face the winters with no style or charm. Odds were, gypsies never even lived in it. It appeared to be a half dugout with a second floor built on years later. The first floor was planted down into the earth a few feet, so the second-floor windows were just above their heads, giving the place the look of a house that had been stepped on by a giant.

Everyone called it the Gypsy House because a group of hippies had squatted there in the seventies. They'd painted a peace sign on one wall, but it had faded and been rained on until it almost looked like a witching sign. No one remembered when the hippies had moved on or who owned the house now, but somewhere in its past a family named Stanley must have lived there because old-timers called it the Stanley house.

"I heard devil worshippers lived here years ago." Tim began making scary-movie-soundtrack noises. "Body parts are probably scattered in the basement. They say once Satan moves in, only the blood of a virgin will wash the place clean."

Reid's laughter sounded nervous. "That leaves me out."

Tim jabbed his friend. "You wish. I say you'll be the first to scream when a dead hand, not connected to a body, touches you."

"Shut up, Tim." Reid's uneasy voice echoed in the night. "You're freaking me out. Besides, there is no basement. It's just a half dugout built into the ground, so we'll find no buried bodies."

Lauren screamed as Reid kicked a low window in, and all the guys laughed.

"You go first, Lucas," Reid ordered. "I'll stand guard."

To Lauren's surprise, Lucas slipped into the space. His feet hit the ground with a thud somewhere in the blackness.

"You next, Tim," Reid announced as if he were the commander.

"Nope. I'll go after you." All Tim's laughter had disappeared. Apparently he'd frightened himself.

"I'll go." Lauren suddenly wanted this entire adventure to be over with. With her luck, animals were wintering in the old place.

"I'll help you down." Reid lowered her into the window space.

As she moved through total darkness, her feet wouldn't quite touch the bottom. For a moment she just hung, afraid to tell Reid to drop her.

Then she felt Lucas's hands at her waist. Slowly he took her weight.

"I'm in," she called back to Reid. He let her hands go, and she dropped against Lucas.

"You all right?" Lucas whispered near her hair.

"This was a dumb idea."

She felt him laugh more than she heard it. "That you talking or the gypsy's advice? Of all the brains dropping in here tonight, yours would probably be the most interesting to take over, so watch out. A ghost might just climb in your head and let free all the secret thoughts you keep inside, Lauren."

He pulled her a foot into the blackness as a letter jacket dropped through the window. His hands circled her waist. She could feel him breathing as Reid finally landed, cussing the darkness. For a moment it seemed all right for Lucas to stay close; then in a blink, he was gone from her side.

Now the tiny flashlight offered Lauren some much-needed light. The house was empty except for an old wire bed frame and a few broken stools. With Reid in the lead, they moved up rickety stairs to the second floor, where shadowy light came from big dirty windows.

Tim hesitated when the floor's boards began to rock as if the entire second story were on some kind of seesaw. He backed down the steps a few feet, letting the others go first. "I don't know if this second story will hold us all." Fear rattled in his voice.

Reid laughed and teased Tim as he stomped across the second floor, making the entire room buck and pitch. "Come on up, Tim. This place is better than a fun house."

Stepping hesitantly on the upstairs floor, Lauren felt Lucas just behind her and knew he was watching over her.

Tim dropped down a few more steps, not wanting to even try.

Lucas backed against the wall between the windows, his hand still brushing Lauren's waist to keep her steady as Reid jumped to make the floor shake. The whole house seemed to moan in pain, like a hundred-year-old man standing up one arthritic joint at a time.

When Reid yelled for Tim to join them, Tim started back up the broken stairs, just before the second floor buckled and crumbled. Tim dropped out of sight as rotten lumber pinned him halfway between floors.

His scream of pain ended Reid's laughter.

In a blink, dust and boards flew as pieces of the roof rained down on them and the second floor vanished below them, board by rotting board.

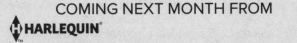

REQUEST YOUR FREE BOOKS!
2 FREE NOVELS PLUS 2 FREE GIFTS!

HARLEQUIN®

American Romance®

LOVE, HOME & HAPPINESS

YES! Please send me 2 FREE Harlequin® American Romance® novels and my 2 FREE gifts (gifts are worth about $10). After receiving them, if I don't wish to receive any more books, I can return the shipping statement marked "cancel." If I don't cancel, I will receive 4 brand-new novels every month and be billed just $4.74 per book in the U.S. or $5.49 per book in Canada. That's a savings of at least 12% off the cover price! It's quite a bargain! Shipping and handling is just 50¢ per book in the U.S. and 75¢ per book in Canada.* I understand that accepting the 2 free books and gifts places me under no obligation to buy anything. I can always return a shipment and cancel at any time. Even if I never buy another book, the two free books and gifts are mine to keep forever.

154/354 HDN GHZZ

Name _____ (PLEASE PRINT) _____

Address _____ Apt. # _____

City _____ State/Prov. _____ Zip/Postal Code _____

Signature (if under 18, a parent or guardian must sign) _____

Mail to the **Reader Service:**
IN U.S.A.: P.O. Box 1867, Buffalo, NY 14240-1867
IN CANADA: P.O. Box 609, Fort Erie, Ontario L2A 5X3

Want to try two free books from another line?
Call 1-800-873-8635 or visit www.ReaderService.com.

* Terms and prices subject to change without notice. Prices do not include applicable taxes. Sales tax applicable in N.Y. Canadian residents will be charged applicable taxes. Offer not valid in Quebec. This offer is limited to one order per household. Not valid for current subscribers to Harlequin American Romance books. All orders subject to credit approval. Credit or debit balances in a customer's account(s) may be offset by any other outstanding balance owed by or to the customer. Please allow 4 to 6 weeks for delivery. Offer available while quantities last.

Your Privacy—The Reader Service is committed to protecting your privacy. Our Privacy Policy is available online at www.ReaderService.com or upon request from the Reader Service.

We make a portion of our mailing list available to reputable third parties that offer products we believe may interest you. If you prefer that we not exchange your name with third parties, or if you wish to clarify or modify your communication preferences, please visit us at www.ReaderService.com/consumerschoice or write to us at Reader Service Preference Service, P.O. Box 9062, Buffalo, NY 14240-9062. Include your complete name and address.

HAR15

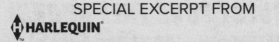
She'd know that butt anywhere. Hunter Boone.

In eleven years, his derriere hadn't changed much. And,
apparently, the view still managed to take her breath away.

"Need some help with that, Josie?" Her father's voice
made her wince.

She was clutching a tray of her dad's famous German
breakfast kolaches and hiding behind the display counter.
Why was she—a rational, professional woman—ducking
behind a bakery counter? Because *he'd* walked in.

She shot her father a look as she said, "Thanks, Dad.
I've got it." Taking a deep breath, she stood slowly and
slid the tray into the display cabinet with care.

"Josie? Josie Stephens?" a high-pitched voice asked.
"Oh my God, look at you. Why, you haven't changed
since high school."

Josie glanced at the woman but couldn't place her, so
she smiled and said, "Thanks. You, too."

That was when her gaze wandered to Hunter. He was
waiting. And, from the look on his face, he *knew* Josie
had no idea who the woman was.

"So it's true?" the woman continued. "Your dad said you were coming to help him, but I couldn't imagine you back *here*. We *all* know how much you hated Stonewall Crossing." Josie remembered her then. Winnie Michaels. "What did you call it, redneck hell—right?" Winnie kept going, teasing—but with a definite edge. "Guess hell froze over."

"Kind of hard to say no when your dad needs you," Josie answered, forcing herself not to snap.

Her father jumped to her defense. "She wasn't about to let her old man try to run this place on his own."

"It's kinda weird to see the two of you standing here." Winnie glanced back and forth between Josie and Hunter. "I mean, without having your tongues down each other's throats and all."

Hunter wasn't smiling anymore. "I've gotta get these to the boys."

Josie saw him take the huge box by the register. A swift kick of disappointment prompted her to blurt out, "Too bad, Hunter. If I remember it correctly, you knew how to kiss a girl."

"If you remember? Ouch." His eyes swept her face, lingering on her lips. "Have fun while you're back in hell, Jo. I'll see you around."

Don't miss
A COWBOY'S CHRISTMAS REUNION
by Sasha Summers,
available in October 2015 wherever
Harlequin® American Romance®
books and ebooks are sold.

www.Harlequin.com

HARFXP0915